I0610008

Thomas Penrose

A Sketch of the Lives and Writings of Dante and Petrarch

with some account of Italian and Latin literature in the fourteenth century

Thomas Penrose

A Sketch of the Lives and Writings of Dante and Petrarch
with some account of Italian and Latin literature in the fourteenth century

ISBN/EAN: 9783337230944

Printed in Europe, USA, Canada, Australia, Japan

Cover: Foto ©Andreas Hilbeck / pixelio.de

More available books at **www.hansebooks.com**

A

S K E T C H

OF THE

LIVES AND WRITINGS

OF

OF THE

LIVES AND WRITINGS

OF

DANTE AND *PETRARCH*.

WITH SOME ACCOUNT OF

ITALIAN AND LATIN LITERATURE

IN THE

FOURTEENTH CENTURY.

Poſſum nonunquam ad illum *Dantem & Petrarcham* alioſque veſtros compluſculos, libenter & cupidè comeſſatum ire nam neque me tam ipſæ Athenæ Atticæ cum illo ſuo pellucido Iliſſo, nec illa vetus Roma ſuâ Tiberis ripâ retinere value-runt, quin ſæpe Arnum veſtrum, & Fæſulanos illos colles inviſere amem.

MILTONI Epiſtol. Epiſt. viii.
B. Bommathæo Florentino.

LONDON:

PRINTED FOR JOHN STOCKDALE, PICCADILLY,

M.DCC.XC.

A

SKETCH

OF THE

LIVES AND WRITINGS

OF

DANTE AND *PETRARCH.*

———————

THE revival of letters [a], and the progress of genius and manners, have ever been dear to the lovers of literature; and when every concomitant circumstance is minutely traced by

[a] It is not intended here to treat of those physical causes which are supposed to have some influence on the progress of arts and literature. The curious reader is referred to the 13th section of the Abbé Du Bos' Reflections on Poetry and Painting; let us only intro-

B   duce

by the hiftorian and antiquary, we are apt to
contemplate with pleafure the ftruggles of ex-
piring barbarity, and the rife of elegance and
polite learning. That Italy fhould be the
country which firft fhewed the fymptoms of an
anxious defire to throw off the fhackles of ignorance, and break the bonds of barbarifm, is
not the leaft furprifing, fince (to ufe the words
of a learned hiftorian), even in the darkeft
periods of monaftic ignorance, fhe had always maintained a greater degree of refinement and knowledge than any other European
country. In the beginning of the fourteenth
century, and at the end of the fixteenth, refinement feemed to exert herfelf with fome degree

duce a remark which he makes on the influence of
climates: " Si Jules II. et Leon X. avoient regné en
" Suede croit-on que leur munificence eût formé dans
" les climats Hiperborées, des Raphaels, des Bembes,
" & des Machiavels ? Tous les Pays font-ils propes à
" produire de grands Poëtes et de grands Peintures ?"

of power; and more particularly in forming, under Leo the Xth, a body of men, who for abilities, learning, and accomplishments, might vie with thofe of the Auguftan age. The great patronage extended to men of learning by a prince, who, to the deeper ftudies of the fcholar, added the polite and refined manners of the courtier, could not fail to draw into being the poet, philofopher, and painter. But as the firft dawn of the morning is often furveyed with as much pleafure as the fun in his meridian brightnefs, the editor will therefore attempt to trace the early productions of Italian poetry, and excufe himfelf from proceeding farther; fince that fubject is likely foon to receive ample illuftration from one of the firft critics of the age. It has been remarked that Europe may perhaps behold ages of a bad tafte, but will never again relapfe into barbarifm :— the fole invention of printing has forbidden

that

that event ^b.; In the fifteenth century, this art,
whofe firft materials were rough, and execu-
tion clumfy, was the means of multiplying
manufcripts, and circulating more freely the
remaining relics of knowledge. Yet many
years before literature received this very valuable acquifition, and any other method of communicating information was conceived, than
that of laborioufly copying old and imper-
fect manufcripts, flourifhed Dante ^c, the Ennius,

^b The firft book which was printed in Italy was in
Italian : it was printed at Venice, by Nicolas Janfon, in
8vo, 233 pages. At the beginning is this note---Quefta
e un' opera la quale fi chiama Decor puellarum : cioe
honore de le donzelle: la quale da regola, forma,
e modo al ftato de le Honefte Donzelle. At the end---
Anno a Chrifti Incarnatione 1461, per Magiftrum Ni-
colaum Jenfon; hoc opus, quod Puellarum Decor dicitur,
feliciter impreffum eft. Laus Deo.

^c He was born in the year 1265, at Florence, of the
families of the Alighieri, and De Bella, whofe connections
we are but flightly acquainted with.

———— and

and father of Italian poetry. After seven hundred years of ignorance and darknefs, when learning, immured in the cloifter, and circumfcribed to narrow limits, was ufelefsly employed in metaphyfical difquifitions, this meteor of genius, as it were, blazed out with redoubled luftre.—Poetry, with her fifter arts, was as yet in a ftate of weaknefs and childhood; rude and uncultivated in her appearance, rough and untutored in her manners, fhe gained but little polifh and refinement from Cicello D' Alcama [d], Lucius Druffe de Pifa [e], or from the regal hands of Frederic II. [f], who, captivated and allured by the charms of literature,

[d] He compofed verfes about the end of the 12th century---the firft Sicilian poet.

[e] He lived in the year 1170, and is cited by Giambullari.

[f] Triffino, Allacci, and Crefcimbeni, have publifhed fome of this prince's love-verfes, which are written in the Sicilian dialect.

cultivated

cultivated in Sicily a taſte for poetry.—To
Dante alone was it given to ſhew to an unenlightened nation the bold and vigorous flights
of a fervid imagination.   The vivacity of his
temper, and the quickneſs of his genius, were
ſtrong recommendations to the famous Brunetto
Latini [g], who, as tutor in the belles lettres, paid
particular attention to his pupil.

The

[g] Villani acquaints us that Brunetto Latini, Dante's
maſter, was the firſt who attempted to poliſh the Florentines, by improving their taſte and ſtyle, which he
did by writing his grand work, the Teſoro, in Pro-
vençal---he died in 1294.   Fu un grande filoſopho (to
uſe the words of his biographer), et fu un ſummo
maeſtro in rettorica, tanto in ben ſaper dire, quanto in
ben dittare: et fu dittatore del noſtro commune; egli
fu cominciatore e maeſtro in digroſſare i Fiorentini, et
furgli ſcorti in bene parlare, et in ſapere, giudicare, e
reggere noſtra republica ſeconda la politica.----El fu
quelli chaſpoſe la rettorica di Tullio, et fece il buono ed
utile libro, detto Teſoro et Teſorato, & la Chiave del
Teſoro, & piu altri libri in filoſofia, et quelli dei vizj

et

The great learning and extenfive erudition of Brunetto were of infinite fervice in adding ftrength

et della virtu.---La Chiave del Teſoro, is a work, I believe, not very well known. In the year 1257, the Rhetoric of Tully was tranflated into Italian by Galiotto Guidotti: it was firft printed in the year 1478, with this title---" Rettorica nova di M. Tullio Cicerone, tranflatata di Latino in volgare per lo enimio maeſtro Galiotto da Bologna." The reaſons why Brunetto choſe to write his Teſoro in French, will be better known by making uſe of his own words :---1ſt, Parceque nouȿ fommes in France. 2d, Parceque la parlure eſt plus delitable, & plus commune a tous langaiſes.---In the library of the Marquis Ricardi at Florence, is a manuſcript Chronicle of Venice, from the foundation till the year 1275, written in French by Maitre Martinda da Canale, who in his introduction fays, as a reafon for uſing that language, Parceque la langue Françoiſe cort parmi le monde eſt la plus delitable á lire et a oir que nulle autre. Befides theſe, who cultivated the Provençal language in preference to the Italian, a Maitre Guillame, a Dominican of Florence, having written a book on the virtues and vices, tranflated it into French in the year 1279, at

B 4 the

ftrength and firmnefs to the flighty genius of
Dante; and from fuch an inftructor it may be
fuppofed that, with a confiderable fhare of critical knowledge, he conceived the idea of
rendering to his country the moft effential fervice in his power, that of purifying and enriching its language. A tafte for poetry was
eafily imbibed from Guido Cavalcanti [h], an
intimate friend, and contemporary writer.
Thefe early feeds were foftered and nourifhed
by the writings of Guido Guinicelli [i], the

great

the defire of Philip the Hardy. Fontanini is miftaken
when he affirms that the Italians wrote in French, in
preference to their own language; it was the Provençal, at that time the moft fafhionable, whofe idioms are
different from the French.

[h] He died in the beginning of the 14th century:---his
poems have been publifhed in a Collection of the Old
Italian Poets, printed at Florence, 1527, 8vo, very fcarce
and curious.

[i] This poet, whofe verfes are to be met with in the old
collections,

great favourite of Dante, who in his Purgatory has honoured him with the title of Father. If we may judge from his work, " De Vulgari Eloquentia," it appears that he was acquainted with moſt of the firſt Italian poets, and by ſmoothing the uncouth phraſeology of theſe early writers, modulated the language, and gave to it a clear and eaſy flow. We will here mention two Italian poets of whom Dante has not taken the leaſt notice, through ignorance.—He has (ſays a very learned and acute critic [k]) mentioned only thoſe who, for their coarſe and inharmonious ſtyle, deſerved reprehenſion—all theſe I will omit, as indifferent verſifiers, and only take notice of a Flo-

collections, flouriſhed about the middle of the thirteenth century.

[k] The improved edition of the Hiſtory of Italian Literature, by Tiraboſchi, will amply ſupply the editor with many intereſting anecdotes in the courſe of this Eſſay.

rentine,

rentine, whofe name and exiftence are hardly
known. Dante de Majano was the poet with
whom Dante Alighieri was totally unacquaint-
ed: to him we muft add Nina of Sicily, the
firft female poet among the Italians[1], between
whom and Dante de Majano a fingular amour
fubfifted; fince, without a perfonal acquaintance, and without once feeing one another,
they continually fent verfes expreffive of love
and regard, which are preferved in the collec-

[1] It has been remarked by an ingenious writer, that
the firft poets have either copied the verfes of women,
or have been inftructed by them---" La Greece qui fe
vante de neuf Poetes Lyriques, fe vante de neuf Dames
excellentes en ce genre de Poefie, et Pindare le Prince
de ces neuf fameux Poetes fut le difciple de Myitis, l'une
de ces dames, et n'eut point de honte d'etre repris de
Corinné, qui en etoit une autre, n'y d'etre vaincu cinq
fois folemnellement par elle. Les Grecques nous affuere-
ront qu'ils ne tiennent leur eloquence que de leur mere,
& Hortenfius nous perfuadera qu'il laiffe fa fille heritiere
de la fienne.   Oeuvres de Sarafin, p. 224.

tion

tion made by Giunti. Nina wifhed to be called the Nina of Dante; and Dante was proud of circulating verfes, which his chimerical affection had dictated in honour of his Sicilian miftrefs. Dante D'Alighieri having now fufficiently cultivated his tafte for poetry, turned his thoughts to deeper and more fevere ftudies: for this purpofe he went to Bologna and Padua[m], from whofe univerfities he gained a ftock of the moft ufeful and inftructive information. Poetry was not the only ftudy of Dante, nor was he fo much captivated and allured by her charms, as to forget the duties

[m] It is from Benvenuto D'Imola that we learn this, as his biographers have not mentioned it; and from Francis Buti (a writer almoft contemporary with Dante, whofe profeffion was to comment on his works, and to interpret them in the univerfity of Pifa and Bologna; during the 14th century), we are told that Dante took the habit of the Fratrum Minorum, an ecclefiaftical order, but left it before he had taken the oaths.

of

of a faithful citizen. His country was as dear
to him as his mufe; and he filled, with equal
honour, the different characters of the poet,
the ftatefman, and the foldier[n]. In the year
1289, warped by the prejudice of party, and
borne along by the prevailing faction of the
Guelfes, he took an active part in the battle
againft the inhabitants of Arezzo, and the fecond year after againft thofe of Pifa.   So
much was he concerned in the affairs of government, that he was fent twice as ambaffador to Charles II. king of Naples ; the firft
time to invite that prince in 1295 to Florence,
where he had been chofen protector of the ftate ;
the fecond, to obtain from the fame prince the
pardon of Vanno Barduci, in whofe caufe the
Florentines ftrenuoufly exerted themfelves. Phi-
lelphes has preferved the fpeeches of Dante on

[n] Æfchylus, whofe genius was as bold and vigorous,
was a poet and a foldier.

that

that occafion ; and the fentence, as repealed by Charles II °. In the year 1300, Dante was chofen prior, or fupreme officer of Florence. This office, it has been fuppofed, was the fource of all his misfortunes, banifhment, and difgrace. The Neri ᴾ, or blacks, as they were called, being affembled in the church of the

ᵒ Dante etant un des Governeurs de la Republique de Florence, avoit fi bonne opinion de fa perfonne, qu'il croioit qu'on ne pouvoit rien faire de bien fans lui, c'eft pourquoi quand il s'agiffoit d'une ambaffadade, il auroit voulu pouvoir la faire, & demeurer en meme tems a Florence, il difoit, " Si io vo, chi fta ? fi io fto, chi va ?" fi j'y vais, qui fera ici ? fi je refte, qui ira ?

Menagiana, tom. iv. p. 221.

ᴾ The Florentines were at that time all Guelfes : Piftoia, a town in the duchy of Tufcany, was diftracted with the factions of the Pancitichi, and Cancellieri ; the chiefs of Florence were fent to check thefe feditions, but their interpofition rather increafed than flopped their proceedings---the nobles were roufed, and the Guelfes feparated into two parties, called the Neri and Bianchi.

bleffed

bleſſed Trinity, were conſulting how they
might introduce Charles of Valois into Florence : Dante, who was at that time prior;
wiſhed rather to be a mediator in the conteſt,
than a principal, and refuſed to give his ſenti-
ments on either ſide.   The Bianchi, or whites,
ſuppoſing that they were meditating the deſtruc-
tion of their party, were inſtantly in arms : the
Neri caught the alarm ; and a conteſt would
have enſued, had not Dante given his advice
that the chiefs of both parties ſhould be baniſh-
ed.   Whilſt Dante was ſent as ambaſſador
to Boniface VIII q, to conſult him concerning

q Boniface in this negotiation ſhewed himſelf rather par-
tial to the Neri, and Charles of Valois ; for which Dante
has placed him, in his Inferno, among the Simoniſts.---Les
Peintres avec le pinceau font des ſatires auſſi bien que les
poetes ; et ſans emprunter le ſecours de la voix, ils pouſſent
des ſanglantes invectives contre leurs ennemis. En faut-il
d'autre temoin que la vengeance que tira Michel Ange de
ce

ing fome method of pacifying Florence,
Charles arrived, routed the Bianchi, and reftored the Neri. The victorious party imme-

ce maitre des ceremonies Meffer Biagio, qu'il plaça en
enfer dans fon jugement univerfel. On peut ajouter a
ce tour celui d' Annibal Carrache, qui pour fe mocquer de
la fotte vanité de fon Frere, le fit reffouvenir de la baffeffe
de fa naiffance, en lui envoyant une petite efquiffe ou il
avoit reprefenté, fa mere que coufoit un habit, et le bon
homme fon pere, qui enfiloit une aiguille avec des lu-
nettes. Carpenteriana, p. 142.—Mr. Walpole fpeaking of
the refentful temper of Frederic Zucchero (a painter in
the reign of Queen Elizabeth), fays that " while he was
employed by Gregory XIII. to paint the Pauline chapel
in the Vatican, he fell out with fome of his Holinefs's
officers ; to be revenged, he painted their portraits with
ears of affes, and expofed the picture publicly over the
gate of St. Luke's church, on the feftival of that Saint,
the patron of painters.----Verrio, quarrelling with Mrs.
Marriot, the houfekeeper at Windfor, drew her picture for one of the furies---this was to gratify his own
paffion. To flatter that of the court, he reprefented Lord
Shaftefbury among the dæmons of faction in St. George's
hall.----Anecdotes of Painting, vol. i. 4to edit. p. 140.

diately

diately banifhed Dante from Florence for two years, fined him 8000 livres, and, on default of payment, confifcated his goods. However fevere this fentence may appear, their fury neverthelefs did not abate. Cante di Gabrielli, in 1302, was commiffioned to examine into the conduct of thofe who were banifhed, and to condemn them as traitors, robbers, and extortioners. Dante, with his companions in exile, was condemned to be burnt alive[r], fhould he ever fall into the hands of his enraged perfecutors. Such was the fury and malice which animated the citizens, in thofe times of difcord and diffention; and fuch the fevere judgment againft a man, who, rather than ftain himfelf with the blood of his neighbour, en-

[r] This circumftance has efcaped all thofe who have ever written concerning Dante. Sr. Savioli of Bologna was the firft who difcovered this inhuman decree; the original of which he found in the archives of Florence in the year 1770.

deavoured

deavoured to foften the rigours of civil war, and eftablifh the firm foundation of a general and lafting peace. After all thefe cruel, and, we may venture to fay, unmerited perfecutions, can it be fuppofed that Dante would tacitly fubmit to poverty and banifhment? After having fruitlefsly endeavoured to obtain pardon by the moft tender and affectionate letters, in 1304 he collected into an army all thofe who had been banifhed from Piftoia and Bologna, and marched to Florence. All their attempts to enter the city were fruftrated: the citizens, accuftomed to arms, repulfed the befiegers, who by this unfortunate attack loft for ever all hopes of being reftored to their country. Dante, chagrined at his difappointment, and overcome with defpair, fled to Verona, and buried all his cares in the family of Alboin, at that time governor of the city, and elder

brother

brother of the great Can*. His misfortunes, his good offices to the ſtate, and laſt, not leaſt, his great and extraordinary abilities, failed not to enſure him a friendly and generous reception. . The gaiety and buffoonery of a court had but few charms for the ſerious and auſtère temper of Dante. A rude and ſevere remark, which perſonally inſulted his protector, was the occaſion (as Petrarch informs us) of his leaving Verona ſo abruptly, and taking refuge in the families of the Marquis Morello Mareſpina, and Boſoſi.—Whilſt his talents and miſ-

---

* So liberal was this prince towards men of genius, however poor and unfortunate, that a gallery in his palace was always open for the reception of illuſtrious, but indigent men. Every one had an apartment ſufficiently furniſhed; a table, not richly, but plentifully, ſtored; and a ſervant in waiting : over the doors of every room were emblematical devices and pictures expreſſing their miſéries and misfortunes. It was this prince whom Petrarch ſtyled " The refuge and aſylum of the indigent."

fortunes

fortunes procured him friends and protectors, he ftill had fome hopes of returning to Florence; and for this purpofe wrote to Henry the Seventh, who was preparing to enter Italy; and examine into the conduct of the Guelfes. In the year 1311 Dante offered his fervices to Henry, animated him with the defire of befieging Florence, and, as if he were certain of fuccefs, indulged himfelf with the moft flattering hopes. Too confident in the powers of his mafter, little did he expect a repulfe. Henry, indolent and inexperienced, only wafted his time under the very walls of Florence, in idle and ufelefs preparations; and his death, which happened foon after, was a blow as fatal to the afpiring hopes of Dante, as it was unexpected. After this unfortunate event, Dante turned himfelf wholly to literature, and the mufes. He travelled from Padua into France,

and

and paffed fome time at Paris[1], where the brilliancy of his imagination, the depth of his learning, and unbounded talents, fhone with unufual luftre. In this univerfity he is faid to have publicly fupported many theological difputations, with great force of argument, and found judgment. On his return to Italy, Gui Novello de Polenta, governor of Ravenna, invited him to his palace; and fo ftrong was his esteem for his unfortunate gueft, that he not only conferred on him the higheft honours, but fent him publicly as his ambaffador to Venice, to conclude a treaty of peace between Ravenna and that city. The Venetians behaved with arrogance, no fubmiffions were re-

[1] Both Boccacio and Dante ftudied at Paris, where they much improved their tafte by reading the fongs of Thiebauld king of Navarre, Gaces Brulés, Chatelain de Coucy, and other ancient French Fabulifts.

Hiftory of Englifh Poetry, vol. i. p. 463.

ceived,

received, and no treaty concluded.   Dante, chagrined and difcontented, returned to Ravenna,
and fhortly after (through vexation, as it is
fuppofed) died at the palace of his friend, on
the 14th of September, in the year 1321, and
the fifty-fixth of his age [u].   His funeral, which
was fuperb and magnificent, was attended by
all the nobles of Ravenna; and the prince himfelf, as the laft duty at the grave of his friend,
pronounced an eulogium over him.   The Venetians, however they had fecretly wifhed for

[u] His ftrength of mind was not the leaft impaired
even in his laft moments; and he is faid to have compofed his own epitaph juft before he expired, in Latin
Leonine hexameters, which I will fubjoin :

Jura Monarchïæ, Superos, Phlegetonta, Lacufque
Luftrando cecini, voluerunt fata quoufque ;
Sed quia pars ceffit melioribus hofpita caftris
Auctoremque fuum petiit, felicior aftris
Hic claudor Danthes patriis extorris ab oris
Quem genuit parvi Florentia mater amoris.

C 3

his

his death, when mafters of Ravenna, erected a
monument to his memory, which, in the year
1692, was rebuilt, and ornamented at the expence of Cardinal Dominic Coffi, at that time
governor of Ravenna.—The Florentines, fenfible of the merits of this illuftrious man, were
now ready to pay thofe honours to him when
dead, which they had refufed when living.
Ambaffadors were fent to Ravenna to beg the
afhes of fo excellent, but unfortunate a citizen; yet fo great was the love for Dante at
Ravenna, and fo valuable did even his remains appear in the eyes of his protectors,
that the folicitations of his countrymen were
rejected [w].   The ardor of the Florentines was

not

[w] There feems indeed to be fomething in poetry that
raifes the poffeffors of that very fingular talent far higher
in the eftimation of the world in general, than thofe
who excel in any other of the refined arts ; and accor-
dingly we find that poets have been diftinguifhed by

antiquity

not to be checked by this refufal; a ftatue of this great ornament of their ftate was carried in triumphal pomp to the church of St. John, and publicly crowned by the prior, amidft the ac-clamations of a grateful and generous people. Medals were caft in honour of his fervices and talents; and the name of Dante was every where mentioned with the higheft applaufe and veneration.

Such was the political character of Dan-te, and fuch were the " many coloured" fcenes of his life.—As a ftatefman we on-ly fee him hurried on by party prejudice, condemned to poverty and banifhment—as a

antiquity with the moft remarkable honours. Thus Homer was deified at Smyrna—as the citizens of Miti-lene ftamped the image of Sappho on their public coin. Anacreon recieved a folemn invitation to fpend his days at Athens; and Hipparchus, the fon of Pififtratus, fitted out a fplendid veffel in order to tranfport him thither.

poet, we look up to him with filial awe and reverence, as to the father of Italian poetry. With his excellences therefore, as a writer, let us clofe thefe remarks.

The rough and inharmonious verfes of the oldeft Sicilian poets [x], the inventors of Ita-

lian

---

[x] The oldeft Italian poetry (fays the learned Mr. Warton) feems to be founded on that of Provence—feveral of Dante's fictions are derived from the fame fountain. Dante has honoured fome of the Troubadours with a feat in his Paradife; and in his tract " De Vulgari Eloquentia," he has mentioned Thiebauld, king of Navarre, as a pattern for writing poetry. To this remark let us add that of the linguift Duret, who fays that fome are of opinion that it came from Sicily, fome from Provence, but does not exactly determine whence it took its origin. " Pour la plus grande molleffe & effemination des Siciliens, on leur attribue la poefie par rythmes et cadences comme auffi ils ont efte les premiers qui ont traicte l'amour en langue vulgaire et en rythme, fi on adjoufte foy a Dante & a Petrarch, bien qu'il y en aye qui attribuent cecy a nos Gaulois, & aux Limofins,

'lian poetry, were compofed as early as the end of the twelfth century. Cicello D' Alcama (as it has been before obferved), Lucius Druffe del Pifa, and Folchacchieri del Siena, being ·the firft who gave any idea of Italian verfe. Frederic the Second, king of Sicily, and his two fons, Euzio king of Sardinia, and Mainfroy king of the two Sicilies, were all untutored votaries of the mufe; but Euzio is faid to have excelled both his father and brother in poetry.—About the middle of the thirteenth century flourifhed Guinicelli, and ·Ghiflieri: the poems of the firft are ftill' to be found in the colleftions of ancient Italian ·poetry; but thofe of the latter, as well· as thofe of Fabricci, are unfortunately loft.

Limofins, & Provençaux ceque je croy, fi on a efgard .a la derniere façon de rythmailler, & de donner nombre aux vers par une mefme fin et definence des voix fur la clofture d'iceux, defquels le Dante a faift un livre, ·que j'ay veu ecrit a la main.

From

From the poems of Cavalcanti [y] (in which, be-
sides the great and evident alteration in the
language, a vein of philofophical morality is
perceptible), Dante derived his tafte for poetry; and, from the rude and early writers of
Sicily, a ftock of words, which, to his nice
and mufical ear, appeared barbarous and dif-
fonant : the great end he therefore propofed to

[y] His fonnet (if we may fo call it) on the love of this
world, is a mafter-piece, confidering the times in which
he wrote : it has been the fubject of many long and
learned commentaries---the ingenious and acute Gilles
of Rome was the firft commentator. In the edition
(fays Bayle) of Sienna, in 1602, fome obfervations of
Celfo Cittadini are added. Efpofizione di Egidio Colonna fopra la Canzone di Amore di Guido Cavalcanti,
&c. &c. in Siena, 1602, in 8vo.---Dino del Garbo of
Florence, an eminent philofopher, followed the example of Gilles. Fran. P. del. Roffo, James Mini, Plinius
Tomacelli, and laftly, Jerom Frachetta, a philofopher of
Rovigo, have commented on it.

Vid. Crefcimbeni, Hift. della Volg. Poef.

himfelf,.

himfelf, and indeed the greateft fervice to his country, was, to new mould and foften the afperities of his native language. Concerning the year in which the Divine Comedy [z] (as he

[z] The reafon why Dante chofe to give it the title of Comedy, has been a fubject of difpute among the learned. The critics rather agree with Maffei and Taffo, who fuppofe that Dante in his ftyle intended to exemplify three kinds of writing—the fublime, he called tragic—the middle, comic---and the third, elegiac : fo that we muft conclude that, by calling it Comedy, he fuppofed that the middle ftyle was generally ufed throughout the poem. Perhaps the Inferno of Dante is the next compofition to the Iliad in point of originality and fublimity ; and, with regard to the pathetic, let this tale (fpeaking of Count Ugolino) ftand a teftimony of his abilities; for my own part, I truly believe it was never carried to a greater height.---Effay on Pope, Vol. i. p. 266. —Francis the Firft forbad the reading of the Inferno in France, becaufe Dante had made Hugh Capet fay---" Figliovol fui d'un Beccaio di Parigi."---Canto XX. of the Purgatory.

See Pafquier's Recherches de la France, p. 452.

called

called it) firſt appeared, many and variout have been the determinations. We are led to ſuppoſe that ſome detached parts were compoſed in the year 1300[a] (a period in which he was engaged in civil war and bloodſhed), rather before his baniſhment; and finiſhed about the year 1311, at the time when, animated with the hopes of returning to his country, he applied to Henry the Seventh. Certain it is that Florence was the place in which he ſketched out a rough draught of his poem; and the more finiſhed parts were compoſed in his leiſure and uninterrupted moments. Many are

[a] It was when Italy was torn in pieces---when the little ſtates were leagued againſt each other---in a word, in the heat of the ſtruggle and bloodſhed of the Guelfe and Gibeline parties, that Dante withdrew from his country, and made the ſtrongeſt draught of men and their paſſions that ſtands in the record of modern poetry.

Enquiry into the Life and Writings of Homer, p. 65.

the

the retreats fuppofed to have been chofen by Dante, for finifhing in peace and tranquillity the remainder of his poem. Udina, Verona, and Ravenna, difpute the honor of having been the feat of the mufes: and in the monaf-tery of Fonta Avellona the chamber is fhewn in which Dante retired to compofe his great and immortal work. The title of Divine has been given only to the works of Homer and Plato; but the judgment of the learned of all nations has given to the Comedy of Dante the fame diftinguifhed title. Though the author wifhed to be the model of the middle-ftyle, he has fhewn how little government he had over his impetuous imagination[b]. He is bold, ma-

jeftic,

---

[b] Although the author of the Effay on Pope has faid that unexemplified criticifm is always ufelefs and abfurd, yet I hope he will pardon me in not citing particular paffages of this fublime writer; as I have lately heard,

and

jeſtic, and ſublime; his vaſt and comprehen-
ſive mind, embracing at once things human
and divine, ſoars as far "as angels ken."
Maſter as he is of poetical beauties and ornaments; he has diſcovered a wonderful knowledge of philoſophy, aſtronomy, theology, hiſtory, politics, and oratory. At times indeed
(and what writer is not?) he is inferior to his
ſubject: his images are ſtrange and unnatu-
ral; his rhymes forced and inharmonious;
his ſtyle harſh and unpoliſhed; his ſtanzas
dull and tedious. But, upon the whole, let us
not forget that in his poem the exalted ideas
of Homer are often clothed in rich and gorgeous trappings; that there is throughout a
vigorous imagination, whoſe grand and ſub-

and I hope with truth, that he is engaged in a Hiſtory
of Italian Literature, from Dante to Metaſtatio : a work
in which I doubt not more taſte, more learning, and
more elegance will be diſplayed, than falls to the lot of
ordinary abilities.

Time

lime conceptions few painters [c] could exprefs, and few poets imitate. The general efteem for the works of Dante was fo great, that it almoft rofe to enthufiafm [d]. Public lectures were inftituted for elucidating and explaining particular paffages of his poem, in imitation of

[c] Michael Angelo Buonarotti, whofe genius was fomething fimilar to that of Dante, had fketched with a pen, on the margin of his copy of the Inferno, every ftriking fcene of the terrible, and pathetic ; but this very valuable curiofity was unfortunately loft in a fhipwreck. It would have been a fingular pleafure to have compared the mafterly fketches of the painter with the more finifhed fcenes of the poet.

[d] The Tufcans were fmitten by the charms of poetry to a greater degree than any other nation, as foon as their language began to be turned towards verfe. One of our old novelifts (Franco Sacchetti, if I remember well) fays that the common people of Florence ufed commonly to fing the poem of Dante about the ftreets, even during the life of that poet, whom we juftly confider is our firft writer of note.—An Account of the Manners and Cuftoms of Italy, by Baretti, vol. ii. p. 174.

thofe

thofe which had formerly been read on the Annals of Ennius. By a decree, on the 9th of Au-
guft 1373, at Florence, Boccacio was appointed to the profefforfhip; and on the third of
October he began his lectures in the church of
Saint Stephen. One of Boccacio's fucceffors
was Philip Villani[e].—Venice, Pifa, and Bologna

[e] Philip Villani, or Villano, muft not be confounded
with his uncle John Villani, nor with his father Matthew Villani.---John has rendered himfelf famous by a
Hiftory of Florence from its foundation to the year
1348, when the plague carried him off. This hiftory
far from being a dry detail, is illuftrated with occafiona
events of other nations; and, that he might make it a
perfect as poffible, he travelled through France and the
Netherlands to collect information. Matthew, his brother, continued it till about the year 1363, when he fell
victim to the plague, which had returned with increafin
violence. Philip, the fon of Matthew, added forty-two
chapters, and afterwards the lives of the illuftrious men
of Florence. The hiftory is written in Italian, and th

logna, followed the example of the Florentines. Benvenuto D'Imola, who held his office fix years, was chofen at Bologna; and, as
lecturer, compofed his Commentary, which
he publifhed at the defire of the Marquis Nicolas the Second, to whom he dedicated it.—
The lecturer chofen by the Pifans was Francis Buti; by the Venetians, Gabriel Squaro
of Verona; and by the univerfity of Plaifance,
Philip del Reggio.

A tafte for Latin poetry was among the leaft
of Dante's accomplifhments; and happily was
it for himfelf and his readers that he abandoned the idea he once entertained of writing his
Inferno in Latin[f]: I fay happily; for although
he

lives in Latin; but Philip, feeing the impropriety of
ufing two languages, tranflated them into Italian, with
little accuracy and faithfulnefs.

[f] In his youth Dante had written his " Vita Nuova," or

he has by his Eclogues convinced us that he
was no defpicable poet in that language, yet
has

the hiftory of his amours with Beatrice, daughter of
F. Portinari, a private gentleman of Florence ; which
contained many poems in praife of his miftrefs, who died
young.   From this Beatrice, whom he has placed in his
Paradife, he receives all his fpiritual leffons in theology.   His Comedy has been tranflated into Latin by Ri-
cardo, a Carmelite ; and by Andreas, a Neapolitan, in
the year 1400 ; and alfo by Paulo Nicoletto, a Venetian,
in 1410.   " Dante defigned at firft that his Inferno, and
Treatife on Monarchy, fhould appear in Latin ; but find-
ing that he could not fo effectually in that language im-
prefs his fatirical ftrokes, or political maxims, on the
laity, or illiterate, he altered his mind, and publifhed
thofe pieces in Italian.   Had Petrarch written his Africa,
his Eclogues, and his profe compofitions, in Italian,
the literature of his country would much fooner have
arrived at Perfection."   Hiftory of Englifh Poetry, vol. i.
p. 147.—With the greateft deference to the learned Mr.
Warton, let us obferve, that his Treatife on Monarchy
was written in Latin, and firft publifhed by Simon
Schardius, at Bafil, 1566, with the title " De Monarchia
Mundi ;"

has he not acquired more honour to himſelf by
enriching and poliſhing the language of his

Mundi;" which, after the death of Dante, was condemned as heretical. His other Latin works (on the authority of Fabricius) were ſome Epiſtles, preſerved' in
La Gàlleria di Minerva at Venice ; in one of which
he ſtiles himſelf a Florentine by birth, not manners;---
Libri duo di Vulgari Eloquentia, publiſhed at Paris,
1575 ; afterwards at Vicenza, 1529 ; tranſlated into Italian by an unknown hand, with a dialogue by John
George Triſſino. Dante della Volgare Eloquenza, *tradot-
to in* Italiano, e publicato da Gio. Giorgio Triſſino—in
Vicenza per Tolomæo Gianicolo, 1529, fol. ; it was re-
publiſhed at Ferrara in 1583, 8vo.---Laſtly, Queſtio de
Natura duorum Elementorum Aquæ et Terræ, publiſhed
by John Benedict Moncetto, at Venice, 1508.---Dante,
poete Italien, a fait trois livres du Paradis, du Purga-
toire, & de l'Enfer, qui ſont une ſatire univerſelle, ou il
drape tout le monde. Il avoit commence ces livres en
Latin par ces vers,

" Pallida regna canam fluido contermina mundo;"
puis il changea d'avis, et les fit en Italien.

Patiniana, p. 87.

D 2   country?

country? by daring to claim to himself a path unknown to his countrymen, and at that time unexplored? and, laftly, by fhaking off the monotonous jingle of the Leonine couplet, and adding grace, harmony, and dignity to the rough and corrupted language of his Gothic anceftors? To Dante therefore, with the utmoft efteem and veneration, is modern Italy to look up, as to one of her greateft ornaments—the author and father of her poetry—who, by his eminent and profound refearches into every branch of fcience, blended the different accomplifhments of the philofopher and poet, and fhewed to the world how much the milder beauties of poetry might gain from the fevere ftudies of abftracted fciences. Poetry, under the hands of Dante, is like a block of marble under the chifel of a Phidias or Praxiteles, which, by the mafterly touches of the artift, is

foon

ſoon reduced to ſymmetry and grace[g].---So intereſting are the lives and charaĉters of men of

[g] To thoſe who are not diſguſted with the perſonal peculiarities of illuſtrious men---and can liſten to Montaigne, when he ſays that he is fond of white wine, without bluntly anſwering, like Mr. Du Puy, What the devil is it to me whether he is or not ?---every minute account of Dante muſt be agreeable. He was, according to his biographers, of a becoming ſtature, but rather inclined to be fat and luſty ; his air was manly and noble, and by his penſive look and continual ſilence aſſumed a kind of ſtern gravity ; his face was long, his eyes large, and his noſe aquiline ; he had broad cheeks, a projeĉting under lip, dark complexion ; a beard and hair long, black, and curling. To beguile his melancholy hours he would frequently amuſe himſelf with drawing---an art in which he had great merit. In converſation he was commonly unintereſting, as he generally ſat in a meditating poſture, and only ſpoke to introduce ſome ſevere, and ſatirical remark. An inſult he never forgot or forgave ; but to his friends and proteĉtors was ever grateful and generous. He was ſo attentive in reading, that Philippus Carolus, in his critique on Aulus Gellius,

gives

of genius, and fo anxious are we to learn the progreffive motions of literature, that every cir-cumftance

gives us a fingular inftance in this paffage---Dantem Flo-rentinum ferunt ad fpectacula ductum, apud bibliopo-lam, quod ex ejus taberna in forum profpectus effet, confediffe, librumque, cujus fuiffet cupidus, inveniffe: quem tam avidè attentèque legerit, ut domum rediens juramento teftatus fit, nihil fe vidiffe, aut audiiffe, ex iis quæ in foro dicta factaque effent.---Giotto the Tufcan, the pupil of Cimabue, painted an exquifite portrait of Dante for the Hotel de Ville at Florence. In the cathe-dral at Florence is a painting of Dante, done by Andrea Orgagna : it was placed there by a decree of the fenate; which decree declares that there fhall be raifed at the public expence, in the cathedral " ed in luogo hono-rato, un marmoreo et artificiofamente fculto fepolchro, con quelle ftatue e fegni che 'lo poteffero rendere orna-tiffimo." The painting is in good prefervation : it re-prefents him walking in a meadow with a book in his hand : in the back-ground is a diftant view of Florence. See a curious book publifhed at Florence, 1783, intitled, " Divini Poetæ Dantis Alighierii fepulchrum a Card. Aloyfio Valenti Gonzago reftitutum." All the ten firft editions

cumftance relating to thefe two points, is generally the fource of entertainment and inftruction.

To the labours and indefatigable enquiries of the Abbé de Sade[h], we are principally
indebted for the many entertaining particulars
relating to Petrarch, whofe extraordinary abilities, and unabating love for Laura, had gained him the approbation and applaufe of Europe.

editions of the Divina Comedia printed from 1472 to
to 1497, are extremely valuable and fcarce; that of 1478,
in which the text is printed in a neat character, and the
commentary in black letter, contains the remarks of
Guido da Terzago, and Jacopo dalla Lana, who are
much efteemed as annotators, but very little known. A
copy on parchment is preferved in the library of the Se-
minary at Padua: Conful Smith was in poffeffion of
another. The edition of 1716 is very valuable; that
of 1731, printed at Lucca, is much efteemed for its explanatory notes; but the beft and moft fuperb edition
is that printed at Venice in 1757, in 5 vols. 4to, ornamented with beautiful engravings.

[h] Memoires pour la Vie de François Petrarch.

Francis

Francis Petrarch was born the 18th of July, at Arezzo [i], in the year 1304. His father, Peter, furnamed Petracco, of a good family, was a notary at Florence [k]; but unfortunately engaging in the conteft of the Neri and Bianchi, was banifhed the city by the victorious party, and in the year 1302 retired to Arezzo, where the Bianchi were fettled. Electa Caningiani, the mother of Petrarch, having permiffion to return

[i] Of the houfe in which he was born, he fays——Anno igitur jubileo Romæ revertenti, atque Aretio tranfeundi, quidam nobiles, qui me comitatu fuo dignum cenfuerunt dum intra mænia urbis adducerent, ignarum me per illum deduxerunt vicum, atque infcio & admiranti domum illam oftenderunt in qua natus effem, haud fane amplam fet magnificam, fed qualis exulem decuiffet.

Epift. iii. Ber. Sen. lib. 13.

[k] However low this occupation may appear, yet fuch was the efteem the Florentines had for Petracco, that they often employed him in the moft important ftations, and more than once fent him as ambaffador to the neighbouring ftates, to negociate peace.

ɔ her native city, carried with her her infant
ɔn, to an eſtate at Ancifa [1], and ſuperintended
·is education till he was ſeven years old. At
his period, when there remained but ·little
ιopes of her huſband's returning to Florence,
he quitted Ancifa, went to Piſa where her huf-
ιand was, thence paſſed by ſea to Marſeilles,
nd laſtly ſettled at Avignon, where the Holy
ſee was eſtabliſhed, and where Petracco after-
ιards engaged himſelf in the ſervice of the
ʔope. At Avignon and Carpentras, Petrarch,
ιith his younger brother Gerrard, applied him-
ιlf to the ſtudy of polite literature [m]; and as

[1] The family of Petrarch was originally of Ancifa, a
rge fortified town, at ſome diſtance from Florence, on
e road to Arezzo.

[m] The fame of Dante being univerſally eſtabliſhed, and
me fragments of the Inferno having accidentally fallen
to his hands, he inſtantly applied himſelf to poetry,
d determined to follow cloſely the ſteps of ſo great a
after.

he

he had difplayed in his early years a ready
and quick apprehenfion, his father, biaffed by
the fordid hopes of a lucrative poft, and determined to wean him from ftudies fo congenial to
his difpofition, fent him firft to Montpelier
and thence to Bologna, for the purpofe of ftu
dying the law. To a mind fo refined and ele
gant, the dry and uninterefting details of Irne
rius muft naturally appear ufelefs and unplea
fant. It was a ftudy, fays Petrarch, for whicl
nature never intended me, and which, at th
death of my father, I totally neglected. Cice
ro, Virgil, and Ovid had for him the moft al-
luring charms; they were the companions o
his leifure moments, and by their affiftanc
his natural propenfity to claffical learning wa
confiderably fupported and increafed. To thefe
his moft favourite authors, was owing a cool
nefs which fubfifted for fome time between hin
and his father, who, from the miftaken idea o

                                        hi

his mifapplication of time, feized his little library [n], and burnt it before his face.   This was

an

[n] Cicero and Virgil, as he himfelf tells us, were faved.
Pater nam memini me tam mœftum contemplatus, fubitò
duos libros, penè jam incendio aduftos, eripuit; et Virgi-
lium .dextrâ tenens, lævâ Rhetoricam Ciceronis, utrum-
que flenti mihi fubridens ipfe porrexit : " Et habe. tibi
hunc (inquit) pro folatio quodam raro animi, hunc pro
adminiculo civilis ftudii."—His tam paucis, 'fed tamen
magnis comitibus animum folatus, lachrymas preffi ; de-
inde circa primos annos adolefcentiæ, mei juris effeftus,
libris legalibus abdicatis, ad folita remeavi : eò ferventior,
quo interrupta deleftatio acrior redit.—Lib. ·xv. Ber.
Sen[m]. Epift. 1.—See an account of the 'lofs of two very
valuable· manufcripts of Cicero, in which was his Treatife on Glory, in the Life of Petrarch, ·by·the ingenious
Mrs. Dobfon —Menage has given us an anecdote concerning the lofs of Cicero's Treatife De Gloria, which I will
tranfcribe, although it has been very fatisfaftorily contra-
·difted by Bayle, under the article Alcyonius. Le traité de
la Gloire de Ciceron fut trouvé tout entier par Philelphe.
Il regarda cette heureufe decouverte comme un moien
de fe faire valoir dans le monde, & d'acquerir une

grande

an infupportable blow to all his literary attain-
ments; and fo ftrongly did he exprefs his for-
row, that his father, moved by his entreaties,
permitted him, at proper intervals, to foften
the feverer ftudies of the law with the perufal of
his favourite authors. In the year 1326, Petrarch, having heard of the death of his father,
quitted Bologna, and arrived at Avignon, juft
time enough to pay his laft duties to his dying
mother. At that time Petrarch (now in his
22d year), together with his brother, entered

grande reputation. C'éft pourquoi il fongea d'abord a le
faire paroitre comme fon propre ouvrage; mais craig-
nant que ce menfonge ne fut découvert dans la fuit-
des tems il fit un traité De Contemptu Mundi, qu'il n-
compofa que des lambaux du livre de Ciceron, qu'i
attacha enfemble du mieux qu'il put: apres quoi i
jetta au feu le traité De la Gloire; et fit perdre a l-
republique des lettres, par cette action odieufe, un ouvrage ou il eft a prefumer qui Ciceron n'etoit pas moin-
admirable, ni moins eloquent que dans fes autres ouvrages.—Tom. iii. p. 163.

into an ecclefiaftical order, for the purpofe of holding a benefice granted to them by the Pope. Petrarch °, ever ftudious of his drefs, and of perfonal elegance, only took the prieft's tonfure, that he might the more indulge himfelf in

° " In the form of Petrarch (fays Jannot Manettus) there was a happy mixture of majefty and grace : he had fo much agility and dexterity that no one could gain the maftery of him." He was extremely well made, and had a very fair complexion ; his converfation was eafy and pleafant ; he never difgufted by an oftentatious difplay of learning, and always gave his opinion with modefty and diffidence. In the expences of his table he was moderate, generally eating fruit, and drinking wine plentifully diluted with water ; and always dined and fupped ftanding. Although temperate himfelf, he was particularly pleafed if any one would call in at dinnertime. Four times in the week he fafted, and on Fridays generally dined on bread and water. He was unufually fearful of thunder and lightning---flept but fhortly, and moft commonly in his clothes. At midnight he arofe to perform the ftated fervices of his order, and afterwards returned to his favourite literary ftudies.

external

external ornaments. " Do you recollect," says he, in a letter to his brother, at that time a Carthusian, " Do you recollect how attentive we were to our dress—how much time we spent in ornamenting our persons—how anxious we were left a blast of wind might derange our curls, and how careful not to discompose the plaits of our gowns?" By this attention to his person, and this vanity in dress, we may natu- rally conclude that he gave himself up more readily to love, and was only studious how he might appear more graceful and elegant in the eyes of a mistress. It was on the 6th of April, on the morning of Good-Friday, in the year 1327, that going to hear the matin-prayers in the church of St. Claire at Avignon, Petrarch for the first time saw the young and beauteous Laura, whose name, whose person, and accom- plishments, have been rendered immortal by the most tender and exquisite verses which the imagination

imagination of a lover could invent. Laura, who at the age only of thirteen had charms sufficient to captivate the heart of Petrarch, muſt have been by nature eminently beautiful, if we can believe the luxuriant deſcriptions of her lover.. But it has been well obſerved that the warm colouring and expreſſive touches of· the poet, muſt give way to the more correct deſign of the painter.ᴾ, who has repreſented her

as.

ᴾ A ſmall portable picture of Laura was painted by Simon de Sienna, an intimate friend of Petrarch. A copy of this picture is now preſerved in the houſe of Sade at Avignon. Laura appears in it, dreſſed in red, holding a flower in her hand, with a ſweet and modeſt countenance, rather inclining to tenderneſs. Under the portico of Notre Dame de Dons is a painting in Freſco much damaged by the weather, but ſufficiently perfect to· diſtinguiſh the figure of Laura dreſſed in green, at the feet of St. George on horſeback, who delivers her from the dragon. In the church of St. Maria Novella at Florence, is an allegorical picture by the ſame artiſt,

in

as of a fair and delicate complexion; her hair
of a light colour; her face round, with a fmall
.forehead,

in which Laura, among the females who reprefented the pleafures of the world, is dreffed in green,
with a little flame rifing from her breaft, her gown em-
broidered with flowers.   At Sienna is fhewn a picture
of the Virgin, which was intended for a portrait of Lau-
ra---in this alfo fhe has a green robe, and her eyes are
fixed on the ground.   An old picture of Laura was
purchafed in 1642, by Cardinal Barberini, which had
been for fome time preferved at Avignon.   In the palace of Turin (fays an entertaining traveller) are two original portraits---one of Petrarch, the other of his be-
loved Laura, by Brongino, a famous painter of that day.
Her fort of beauty would never have captivated me, had
I been Petrarch---firft, her hair is red; her eyebrows extremely narrow, and exactly forming a flat arch; her
eyes fmall; her nofe a little hooked, and rifing too high
in the middle; her mouth not very fmall, and lips like
two fcarlet threads; a very faint colour in her cheeks;
the contour of the face more fquare than oval; her countenance more demure than engaging; her head is covered
with a kind of caul, which fits clofe, and is of gold
net,

forehead, and cheeks rather full; her eyes much cast down, and almost closed—the whole countenance seems to express the modest simplicity of a young girl of a mild disposition and extreme bashfulness. The meek and reserved temper of Laura, was, in the eyes of Petrarch, a virtue worthy of esteem and veneration : but at the same time that he admired the endowments of her mind, he was not blind to the beauties of

net, with pearls of precious stones fastened on in lozenges : this caul confines her hair, excepting a border or roll, which is left all round close to her face. Her gown, which I imagine was intended to imitate embroidery of that day, looks now like a piece of an old Turkey carpet; it is without plaits. Two rows of large pearls, intermixed with rubies and emeralds, hang about her. neck.---I give you this detail of her dress, as it was probably the fashion of her day, and I suppose was esteemed extremely becoming. As for Petrarch, he is exceedingly ugly indeed, but has a very sensible black and yellow face.---Letters from Italy, in the Years 1770 and 1771, by Lady Miller, vol. i. p. 119.

E

her

her perſon; and, by indulging himſelf in the pleaſing conceptions of his imagination, we may not be ſurpriſed if he compared her to the faultleſs beings of another world. Some there are who, in the characters of Petrarch and Laura, have diſcovered the debauchee and the harlot; and have even inſinuated that Clement the Sixth, informed of the improper correſpondence of theſe lovers, had threatened Petrarch with excommunication, unleſs he married Laura [q], whom it was ſuppoſed

[q] Alexander Velutello, who lived in the 16th century, not content with the opinions of the learned concerning the family of Laura, went purpoſely to enquire at Avignon. He ſearched all the regiſters, to find out when ſhe was baptized, and when buried; copied all the pedigrees of the noble families of the country; and, after all his indefatigable enquiries and expenſive journies, he flattered himſelf that he had diſcovered that Laura was the daughter of Henry de Chabeau, a Lord of Cabreria, and that ſhe was baptized the

fuppofed he had debauched: while others, verging on to the extremity of prudery, have conceived that the love of Petrarch was merely platonic, and perfectly philofo-

the 4th of June, 1314. Louis Beccadelli, afterwards archbifhop of Ragufa, wifhing to follow the example of Velutello, and to profit by the difcovery of Laura's tomb, in the church of the Cordeliers at Avignon, in the year 1333, fpent his time in many fruitlefs attempts in this purfuit, and many ufelefs enquiries. At laft Mr. l'Abbé de Sade, whom this difcovery of the tomb perfonally interefted, proved that Laura was the daughter of the Chevalier Audebert de Noves, a magiftrate of Avignon—that fhe was born about the year 1308, in the fuburbs of that town ; and in the year 1325 married to Huques, fon of Paul Sade. In an elegant pamphlet, publifhed, I believe, about three years ago (for I have not feen it lately), intitled, An Effay on the Life and Character of Petrarch, the curious reader will meet with fome very ftrong and ingenious arguments which prove that Laura never was married ; and Velutello himfelf fays, " Per cofa certa habbiamo da tenere che non foffe " maimaritata."

E 2

phical;

phical; founded only on the virtues of the
heart, and the intellectual powers of the mind.
But fay, ye cold and phlegmatic definers of
love! was it to the accomplishments of the
mind that Petrarch paid such tender and fervid
devotion? Could such warm and enthusiastic
raptures, such expressions of love (by some
deemed metaphyfical), be wasted on mere men-
tal talents, however useful and excellent, in a
woman? It was indeed a passion as lasting as it
was vehement; and the more Laura seemed to
check the ardent tranfports of her lover, the
more impetuous was he in his expressions, the
more animated in his poetry. That she would
sometimes bestow on him marks of her esteem
and regard, at those moments when love and
pity had some afcendant over her, is very evident from many parts of his fonnets; and at
these blest intervals Petrarch breaks forth with
raptures the moft expreffive of his short and mo-

mentary

mentary happinefs. Petrarch, loft to the re-
pofe of peace and folitude, and abandoned to
the moft poignant fenfations of love, had long
endeavoured to ftifle a paffion which for fo
many years had been foftered with the tendereft
hopes : a retrofpect of the time that was paft,
confumed in idle and ufelefs anxiety, was even
painful and gloomy. With the determination
therefore of banifhing from his mind the too
ftrongly impreffed idea of his Laura, and devoting the remaining years of his life to the ftudy
of polite literature, he broke away abruptly
from Avignon ʳ, and travelled through France,
Germany,

ʳ The beauty of Laura, in the mean time, drew
daily to Avignon a crowd of ftrangers, anxious to view
the beautiful form of her, who had infpired the firft
of poets with the moft exquifite and pathetic fentiments. Petrarch himfelf fays of her, that " in all the
converfations he ever held with her, fhe remonftrated
with him on the fruitleffnefs of his paffion ; and, rather

E 3   than

Germany, and Italy, with earnest hopes of abandoning for ever the dearest object of his affections. Ever restless and unsettled, he wandered from country to country; and endeavoured, by mixing with the families of other nations, to wean himself from a passion, which, to his sorrow, he found firm and immovable. In 1330, having past part of the year in England, he returned to Avignon, with the bishop Colonna, between whose brother and Petrarch a sincere friendship subsisted. However foreign courts and foreign manners might have pleased and attracted him, Petrarch could not root out entirely from his breast the subtle poison of love and admiration. His absence from Laura served only to heighten his passion; and even the supposition of her favouring the addresses of other suitors, made her appear more

than seem to favour his addresses, endeavoured to excite him to other pursuits."

lovely

lovely and beautiful. At his return, chagrined perhaps at her coolnefs and referve, he bade adieu to the gaieties of Avignon, and retired to the beautiful fpot of Valclufia, where he fought to bury, in peace and folitude, the increafing violence of his attachment. But not even in this favourite retreat could his imagination abandon his amiable Laura. Some of the moft tender of his fonnets were written in his retirement, when his fancy, heated with the idea of his abfent miftrefs, and having its free courfe, poured forth itfelf in complaints, with which (fays he) the vallies, and even the air itfelf, refounded. In 1334, at this feat of the Mufes, Petrarch began a Latin poem, in honor of Scipio Africanus, which he intitled Africa[s],

.and

---

[s] When Petrarch wrote his Africa, he had not feen Silius Italicus. I will add the opinion of Boccacio on this poem---Efto ævo noftro tertius exfurgat Africanus,

non

and which he finifhed after he had received the
laureat's crown. An epic poem, however indifferent,.

non minori gloriâ, majori tamen juftitiâ delatus in æthe-
ra, verfu viri celeberrimi Francifci Petrarchæ, nuper
laureâ Romæ infigniti ; tantâ enim facundiâ & lepiditate
fermonis in medium trahitur, ut ferè ex tenebris longi
filentii in ampliffimam lucem deduƈtus videatur.---That
Petrarch himfelf had but a mean opinion of this poem,
we may judge from the following anecdote---When he
was at Verona, a great concourfe of people affembled to ·
behold fo extraordinary a man : fome among the crowd,
with the hopes of pleafing him, began to recite parts ·
of his Africa; but Petrarch burft into tears, and en-
treated them to defift; adding, that it would be his
greateft pleafure to burn with his own hands fo unfinifh-
ed a work: In the life of Petrarch before cited, the au-
thorefs has faid, " It feems extraordinary that Petrarch
fhould never have fhewn Boccacio a poem he had fpent
fo much time in compofing." It appears very evident,
by this fhort eulogium of Boccacio, that he *had* feen the
Africa, fince he fays, " F. Petrarchæ *nuper* laureâ Romæ
infigniti." In 1341 Petrarch was crowned, and in 1375
Boccacio died, one year after Petrarch. If Boccacio had

never

different, in thofe days of ignorance was efteemed a prodigy. No fooner had Petrarch fhewn the firft fketch, and fome fragments of it, to his friends, than copies were eagerly circulated, and the defire of every one to read fuch an aftonifhing performance was readily excited. This poem, and other Latin works which he wrote about that time, although infinitely inferior to the chafte ftyle of Tully or Virgil, yet, upon the whole, were the beft examples of modern Latinity fince Claudian. The Italians, fenfible of the magnificence of their anceftors, and proud of the name of Petrarch, determined to revive the games in the Capitol, and confer the laureate's crown on the moft eminent poet of their nation[t]. The fenators of Rome, ftruck

with

never feen the Africa till after the death of Petrarch, he would hardly have faid *nuper*, after the lapfe of 34 years.

[t] Hodierno die, horâ fermè tertiâ, litteræ fenatus mihi

redditæ

with the admiration which all Europe had for the merits of Petrarch, and animated with the earnest exhortations of Robert king of Naples, and the bishop Colonna, sent an invitation to him to accept of this distinguished honour. On the same day he received a letter from Robert de Bardi, Chancellor of the University of Paris, begging him to repair thither for the same purpose[u]. He gave the preference to Rome,

as

redditæ sunt; in quibus obnixè admodum, et multis persuasionibus, ad percipiendam lauream poeticam Romam vocor. Eodem hoc ipso die, circa horam decimam, super eâdem re, ab illustri viro Roberto, studii Parisiensis Cancellario, concive meo, mihique et rebus meis amicissimo, nuncius cum litteris ad me venit. Ille me exquisitissimis rationibus ut eam Parisium hortatur. Urget enim hinc novitatis gratia, hinc reverentia vetustatis, hinc amicus, hinc patria.—Epist. Thomæ Messanensi.

[u] Certatim duæ maximæ urbes expofcerent, Roma atque Parisius, altera mundi caput & urbium regina, nutrix alteræ

as the moſt celebrated city in the world. So modeſt was he, and ſo little ſenſible of the extraordinary talents which he poſſeſſed, that he determined to go to Naples, that he might be examined whether he was worthy of ſuch high honours or not. Eaſter-day, in 1341, was the time appointed for this feſtival[w]. Petrarch,

tera noſtri temporis ſtudiorum. Poſt varias deliberationes, ad extremum non alibi quam Roma, ſuper cineribus antiquorum vatum inque iIlorum ſede, percipere, ingenti alios fratre tuo ſuaſore & conſultore, diſpoſui, hoc ipſo die iter aggredi. In quo pluſculum temporis exigitur; adeundusenim rex, videnda Parthenope, inde iter erit Romam.

[w] Senuccio-del Bene, a poet of Florence, who was an eye-witneſs, thus deſcribes this public ſolemnity---Petrarch, clothed in a velvet robe of violet colour, and bound with a zone of diamonds, was conveyed in a triumphal car to the Capitol; and there, amidſt the applauſe of an innumerable multitude, was preſented with three crowns, of laurel, ivy, and myrtle.

See F. Petrarchæ Epiſt. Sec. lib. v. Ren. Sen.

led

led in triumphal proceffion to the Capitol ˣ, was
crowned with a wreath of laurel by the fenator
Orfo del Anquillara, amidſt the acclamations
of the people of Rome.

After this feſtival Petrarch went to Parma,
and ſtaid fome time in the family of the Corre-
gos, by whofe intereſt he gained the archdea-

ˣ Idibus Aprilis, anno ætatis hujus ultimæ 1341, in Ca-
pitolio Romæ, magnâ populi frequentiâ, et ingenti guadio,
peraċtum eſt quod nudius tertius de me Rex apud Ne-
apolim decreverat. Urfus Anquillariæ comes, ac fenator,
præalti vir ingenii, regio judicio probatum laureis fron-
dibus infignivit. After this he adds an anecdote of his
being robbed, which I will not omit—Cætera fupra fpem
et fupra fidem fucceſſiſſe noveris : at, ut recenti experi-
mento cognofcerem quam lætis junċta fint triſtia, vix
mænia urbis egreſſi, ego cum his qui me terrâ et pelago
fecuti erant, in latronum armatas manus incidimus,
e quibus ut liberati, et Romam redire compulfi fumus :
quantufque ibi ob hanc caufam populi motus ! et ut die
poſtero certiori armatorum fulti præfidio difceſſimus, ac
cæteros viæ cafus fi explicare tentavero, longa erit hiſto-
ria.---Epiſtᵃ. Secᵉ. Barbato Sulmonenfi.

conry of Parma, at that time vacant. In 1342, Clement the Sixth being elected Pope, Petrarch, and the famous Gabrina (more commonly known by the name of Cola del Rienzi), were deputed as ambaffadors to carry the complimentary letters. Clement, a profeffed admirer of Petrarch, conferred on him a rich priory near Pifa, and wifhed to create him his apoftolical fecretary; but Petrarch, ever a foe to reftriction and confinement, begged to be excufed from accepting this important office. It was at this period, furrounded with friends and protectors, whofe inclination and ftudy it was to render him every poffible fervice, that he loft his beft and moft illuftrious patron, bifhop Colonna; and, as if it was by the decree of heaven that his happinefs fhould be embittered with the moft poignant affliction, the news of the untimely death of his miftrefs reached him at Parma. On the 6th of April 13:7, the fame day and the fame

hour

hour when, one-and-twenty years before, she was
firſt ſeen by Petrarch, died the beauteous and
accompliſhed Laura.. This melancholy event,
which Petrarch had foreſeen, and which his
miſtreſs, not cheerful as uſual, but pale and
weeping, had announced to him in a dream,
happened whilſt he was at Verona.   The exceſs
of his grief will·be eaſily conceived by thoſe
whoſe feelings are awake to the warm glow of
ſympathy; ſince, even to the cold and inani-
mate heart, the pen of an hiſtorian can give no
adequate idea ʸ.   The ſonnets which he compoſed after her death,. to beguile the melancho-

ʸ Who can read· theſe lines without wiſhing to know
what beautiful and lovely form is the ſubjeết of ſuch ten--
der expreſſions ?

      ——— Lampeggiar del' angelico riſo
    Che ſole an far in terra un paradiſo
    Poca polvere ſon, che nulla ſente
    Ed io pur vivo !
            Sonnet 252.·

ly hours, where he so pathetically laments the loss of this his dearest and most valuable treasure, are conceived and executed with the highest elegance and expression. To the chilled and benumbed apathist the marvellous tenderness of Petrarch appears tame and insipid. But it is not to these that the poet makes his appeal; it is to the compassionate heart, which can be forcibly affected with the tender emotions of sensibility. Petrarch, fixed as it were with the shock, spent the remainder of the year at Parma, in inexpressible sorrow. The contemplation of his misfortunes seemed to have entirely engaged his thoughts; but, sensible of his too firm attachment to an object which existed only in imagination, he endeavoured, by a tour into Italy, to dissipate the cloud of sorrow which loured over him. After having visited Rome and Florence, he returned to Valclusia,.

the.

.the feat of folitude and the Mufes [z]; but the fight of this favourite retreat, and the well-known profpect of Avignon, opened anew the wounds of affliction, and reftored the image of his departed Laura.   At the death of Cle-ment the Sixth [a], which happened in 1352, In-

nocent

[z] Valle, che de'lamenti miei fe' piena,
Fiume, che fpeffo delmio pianger crefci,
Fere filveftre, vaghi augelli, e pefci
Che l'una, e l'altra verde riva affrena;
Aria de' miei fofpir calda, e ferena,
Dolce fentier, che fi amaro riefci
Colle, che mi piacefti, hor mi rincrefci,
Ou' ancor per ufanza amor mi mena,
Ben riconofco in voi l'ufate forme,
Non laffo in me, che da fi lieta vita
Son fatto albergo d'infinita doglia.
Quinci vedea 'l mio bene, e per queft' orme
Torno à veder, ond' al ciel nuda è gita
Lafciando in terra la fua bella fpoglia.

Sonnet 261.

[a] The very vehement invectives and fevere farcafm
whic

ʃocent the Sixth was elected to the papal chair;
and ſo indifferent was he in every thing that re--

which Petrarch is continually throwing out againſt
phyſicians, may be eaſily accounted for.   Clement being
dangerouſly, ill, and wiſhing to follow the advice of the
eminent phyſicians, Petrarch, warning him of his dan-
ger if he truſted to different opinions, deſired him to
chooſe only one, whom he knew to be faithful and
well informed.   The perſon by whom he ſent this
meſſage making ſome miſtake, Clement deſired Petrarch to ſend him his opinion in writing.   The letter
unfortunately falling into the hands of the Pope's chief
phyſician, he was highly incenſed at this inſult, which
he ſuppoſed was intended for the whole profeſſion,
and inſtantly returned a moſt cutting and ſevere an--
ſwer.   This drew from Petrarch all thoſe bitter ſtrokes
of ridicule and contempt which are occaſionally intro--
duced in his Letters; and which firmly fixed that aver--
ſion which he ever had to the ſtudy and profeſſors of
phyſic.---Petrarque etoit grand ennemi (ſays Menage) des
medécins, ſur les mots, " Ars longa vita brevis," qui
ſont au commencement des Aphoriſmes d'Hippocrate, il
dit d'eux que, vitam dum brevem dixerunt, breviſſi-
mam effecerunt.

F   garded

garded literature, and fo weak in underftand-
ing, that he fufpected Petrarch to be a magician [b].   The friends of the injured poet advifed
him inftantly to undeceive the Pope, by going
to him in perfon; but he, neglecting their ad
vice, and defpifing the fuppofitions of this pre
judiced prince, chofe rather to quit Valclufia
and return to Italy.   At Milan he was detain
ed by the archbifhop John Vifconti, who fen
him as his ambaffador, in 1354, to Venice, on
a treaty of peace.   Petrarch, difappointed i
his hopes, returned to Milan, and thence wen
to Mantua, at the requeft of Charles the Fourth
who received him with the moft flattering
marks of efteem, and wifhed him to accompa
ny the court to Rome; but this honor Petrarc
refufed.   In a letter to Charles [c], he remon

[b] Virgil, the great favourite of Petrarch, was fup
pofed to ftudy the dark fcience of witchcraft.

[c] See his printed letter in his fecond book de Vi
Solitariâ.

ftrated with him on the folly of his journey, and his want of attention to the diforders of the ftate ; but fo far was the emperor from correcting this liberty, that he ftill honored him with his correfpondence, and conferred on him the titular honor of Count Palatine. All thefe pofts and preferments, although high and lucrative, were only the fource of trouble and fatigue. To Petrarch the tumult of a court was far from agreeable ; and that he might enjoy retirement, fo congenial to his foul, he chofe a fpot called Linternum, which belonged to the family of the Vifconti, where he fpent the greateft part of his time in reading, walking, and frequently paying vifits to his patron. In 1360, Petrarch, at the requeft of Vifconti, went as ambaffador to Paris, to compliment John II. on his return from England, and acceffion to the throne. John, a lover and protector of the mufes (whofe difpofition was to-

tally

tally unlike that of his turbulent father Philip),
received him with careffes,. and treated him
with the moft friendly marks of hofpitality.
At his return from Paris he received an invitation to the court of the emperor Charles ; but
this he refufed, pleading,. as an excufe, his age
and infirmities.. It was not from Charles that
Petrarch wifhed for honors and riches, for of
thefe he had fufficient; it was a remedy for the
miferies and misfortunes of his country. However weak in other refpects, Charles fupported,
with honor to himfelf, a firm and inviolable
friendfhip for Petrarch ; and, as a prefent at
the birth of his fon, in 1361, fent him a goblet
of gold, of great value and exquifite workman-
fhip.. The fame year he received an invitation
to the courts of John king of France, and
Pope Innocent the Sixth;. but from both thefe
he modeftly excufed himfelf: and, in a letter to
Cardinal de Taillerand, he mentions how great-

ly

ly he was furprifed that a pope, who was fo weak as to fuppofe him a magician, could with any confiftency offer him the poft of Apoftolical Secretary. Padua, Milan, and Venice, were the places chofen by Petrarch for his fummer refidence. At Ferrara, from the Marquis Nicolas the Second, he received diftinguifhed honors; and at laft retired to the beautiful town of Arqua, celebrated by the refidence and death of Petrarch, which happened on the evening of the 18th of July, 1374.—He had retired to his ftudy, as ufual; and was found the next day dead, with his head refting on a book.

Thus, full of years and glory, died Francis Petrarch, the moft learned and accomplifhed fcholar of the age.—His funeral obfequies were, like Dante's, conducted with the utmoft magnificence. The bifhops of Padua, Vicenza, Verona, and Trevifa, perfonally affifted in the ceremony. The nobility and uni-

F 3

verfity

verfity of Padua attended in a body ; and the pall, which was of cloth of gold, fringed with two rows of lace and ermine, was fupported by fixteen doctors of the univerfity. Bonaventure de Peraga, an intimate friend of Petrarch, pronounced the funeral oration over the body, which was interred in the church of Arqua, where a tomb of red marble was afterwards built, with columns in the old tafte, of which Petrarch had been a profeffed admirer [d].

[d] On this tomb were engraved thefe three Latin verfes, written by Petrarch :

Frigida Francifci tegit hic lapis offa Petrarchæ.
Sufcipe, Virgo parens, animam ; fate Virgine, parce!
Feffaque jam terris, cœli requiefcat in arce.

In 1667 Paul de Valdezucchi, proprietor of Petrarch's houfe at Arqua, had his buft in bronze placed on this maufoleum. In 1630 fome perfons broke into this tomb, and took away fome of Petrarch's bones to fell them. The fenate of Venice, enraged at this facrilege, punifhed thofe who were guilty of it with extreme feverity.—Life of Petrarch, vol. ii. p. 544.

In his youth, Petrarch, ever a votary to love, had two children, the mother of whom is not known, but fuppofed to have been of noble family. The eldeft, a fon, died at Verona, in 1361, aged 24 years—the other, a daughter, named Frances, born, according to the Abbé de Sade, in 1348, was married to Francis Broffano, whom Petrarch in his will appointed his heir.—Whether Petrarch thought himfelf poor, or whether it is through modefty that he fays in his will, "Prædicti autem amici de parvitate "hujufmodi legatorum non me accufent, fed "fortunam," I leave to the reader to determine.—But if we examine his will, we fhall find that, confidering the times in which he lived, and the neceffary expences of his many journeys, his many and valuable ecclefiaftical preferments, he muft have been worth confiderable property.

The chief legacies in his will are as follows : "Lego autem ecclefiæ Paduæ ducatos ducentos

auri,

auri, ad emendum aliquantulum terræ. Lego
autem ecclefiæ apud quam fepeliar ducatos viginti; aliis autem ecclefiis quatuor ordinum
Mendicantium, fi ibi fuerint, ducatos quinque
pro quâlibet. Pauperibus Chrifti lego centum
ducatos diftribuendos; ita tamen, ut de dicta
quantitate nulla ultra fingulos ducatos accipiat.
Magnifico domino meo Pæduano (Francifco de
Carrariæ), quia ipfe per Dei gratiam non eget,.
et ego nihil habeo dignum fe, dimitto tabulam
meam, five iconam, B. Mariæ, operis Joctii[d] pic-
toris egregii. De equis meis, fi quos habuero
in tempore tranfitûs mei qui placeant, Bonza-
nello di Vicentiæ, et Lorbardo a Serico, con-.
civibus Paduanis, volo quod inter eos fortian-
tur; et, præter hoc, dicto Lorbardo, qui rerum
fuarum curam depofuit, ut meas res ageret,
obligatum me confiteor in 134 ducatis auri, et
folidis 16, quos expendit in utilitatibus meis, &

[d] i. e. Giotto.

multe

:multo amplius. Item lego eidem Lorbardo
cyphum meum, parvum, rotundum, argenteum
& auratum, cum quo bibat aquam, quam libenter bibit, multo libentius quam vinum.
Presbytero Joanni a Bocheta, custodi Ecclesiæ
nostræ, breviarium meum magnum, quod Vene-
tiis emi pretio centum librarum. Domino de
Certaldo, seu Boccatio, verecundè admodum
tanto viro, tam modicum lego quinquaginta
florenos auri de Florentiâ, pro unâ veste hye-
mali, ad studium, lucubrationesque nocturnas.
Magistro T. Bambasiæ de Ferrara lego leutam
meum bonum. Magistro Joanni de Horologio,
physico, lego quinquagintos ducatos auri, pro
emendo sibi unum parvum annulum digito ges-
tandum, in memoriam mei. De familiaribus
autem domesticis sic ordino: Barthol². de Se-
nis, viginti ducatos; Zilio de Florentiæ, domi-
cillo meo, supra salarium suum, si quid debetur,
viginti ducatos: et si haberem plures, aut alios

- plures

plures pauciorefve domicillòs, fupra falarium fuum, pro quolibet, florenos feu ducatos viginti; famulis duos pro quolibet; coquo duos. Omnium fanè bonorum mobilium & immobilium quæ habeo, vel habiturus fum, ubicunque funt vel erunt, unum folum heredem inftituo Francifcolùm de Borfano, filium quondam domini Amicoli de Borfano, civem Mediolani."

By the death of Petrarch, Italian poetry, and literature in general, fuffered a fevere and lafting fhock. It was owing to him that a tafte for the mufes was more generally diffufed throughout Italy, and the lofs of Dante compenfated by his eminent talents. The language of Italy, at this period, began to affume new beauties; but fo little did Petrarch fuppofe that his fonnets were the caufe of this change, that he fays in one of them (P. II. 252), " If I had conceived that thefe poetical complaints would have been fo much efteemed, I would have

compofed

compofed more, and in a better ftyle^e." By this it appears that unlefs love had infpired him with fuch melancholy ftrains, Petrarch would hardly have exercifed his genius on indifferent fubjects, fince he was only excited to it by his paffion, and in his poetry fpoke only the language of his heart; for, as his countryman fays,

> Amor primà trovò le rime, e verfi,
> E fuoni, e canti, ed ogni melodio.

The firft dawnings of revived literature appeared in the metrical romances of the Troubadours, or Provençal poets, which, although written in a language compofed of Latin and Gaulic, were neverthelefs adapted to catch the attention of the illiterate by the pompous defcriptions of heroes, tournaments, feafts, and triumphs; and among thofe of a more polifhed mind were con-

* La langue Italienne (fays Cardinal Perron) eft fort propre pour la chofes d'amour; a caufe de la quantité de diminutifs qu' elle poffede.

fidered

fidered as evident marks of a bright and vigorous imagination. From thefe minftrels a tafte
for poetry was infenfibly caught by the neighbouring nations; and by the imitation of their
fubject and ftyl., in Italy and England, the
progrefs of poetry may be fuppofed to gain confiderable ftrength and vigour.—" Thefe fables
(fays a learned writer) were an image of the
manners, cuftoms, modes of life, and favourite
amufements, which now prevailed not only in
France, but in England; accompanied with all
the decorations which fancy could invent, and
recommended by the graces of romantic fiction.
They complimented the ruling paffion of the
times; and cherifhed, in a high degree, the
fafhionable fentiments of ideal honor, and fan-
taftic fortitude."—The imaginations of thefe
bards, ftruck with the gorgeous pageantry of
regal feftivals, the fplendor and riches of ori-
ental cities, and the greateft fcene of war and
                                    flaughter

flaughter that modern times had yet exhibited, gave to their romantic fiction a rich glow of imagery, and clothed in the moft pompous ornaments their extravagant ideas of love and valour. The language of thefe poets was fo generally underftood, that Brunetto Latini chofe rather to make ufe of it, than write in the inharmonious tongue of his own country. That there were fome however who only imitated the Provençal poets in ftyle, and not language, has been before mentioned; but to the account of thofe bards let us add, that, after Folchetto, a native of Geneva, had rendered himfelf illuftrious among the Troubadours at Marfeilles, an enthufiaftic ardor inftantly fpread itfelf over Italy, and a conteft for fuperiority in this fpecies of writing roufed the imagination. In the Vatican, and library of Modena, are preferved manufcripts of the lives of Boniface Calvi, a Genevefe, and Bartholomew Georgi, a Venetian,

tian, both Troubadours of eminence. Thefe poets wrote on the war which at that time fubfifted between Venice and Geneva, and in a manufcript at Modena their verfes are preferved. To thefe may be added Sordello, a man of rank at Mantua, who flourifhed about the middle of the 13th century : he was particularly well fkilled in Provençal poetry; and, according to Dante, fpoke the Italian language with fluency. The poetry of Italy we may confider as taking its ftyle, though not its rife, from France ; and in the hands of Guido Guinicelli, Cavalcanti, Guitton d'Arezzo, and laftly Dante, confiderably foftened and improved.

Concerning the firft introduction of metre into Italian poetry, let us cite a paffage from Claude Duret's curious Hiftory of Languages. Le Veluteglio, en fes commentaires en langue Italienne, fur les triomphes de Petrarque ecrivent

ecrivent qui les rythmes Italiennes, et façon de compofer par fonnets, & ftances eft provenue, et procedu, felon aucuns, des Siciliens, lorfqu'un Guillame Ferrabrach, frere de Robert Guifchard, et autres feigneurs de Calabre & Pouille, enfans de Tancred Francois-Normand, les porterent de la provence en Sicile, pays d'Italie, & qu'en ce temps les François s'ayderent de cefte forme & façon de compofer felon la rapport de Francois Petrarque, en la preface de ces Epitres. Les autres difent que cette façon de compofer rythme, fonnets, & ftances, eft provenue des Hetruriens, defquels eft emane le premier et plus ancien language Tufcan : Nos François veulent que cela eft procede de l'invention des poetes Provençaux, qui floriffoient environ l'an de falut 1162, ainfi que l'ont bien remarque Colotius & Bembus, en leur difcours de cette matiere (p. 819).—That rhyme was ufed by the Troubadours, is an eftablifhed fact ; but

that

that it was firſt uſed in the Leonine verſes [f],
which exiſted long before thoſe of Provence,
is, we are led to conjecture, indiſputable.
Rhyme therefore, whether in Latin or French,
is ſuppoſed to have been uſed in Sicily, and
thence tranſplanted into Italy.——Concerning the
ſtate of Latin literature, before and at the time
of Petrarch, let us add a few curſory remarks.
When the empire of Rome fell a prey to the
repeated attacks of the northern nations; and,
flooded as it were with a torrent of barbariſm [g],

the

[f] Some have falſely ſuppoſed that Leonius, a Latin
poet in the 12th century, canon of Paris, who wrote
the greateſt part of the Old Teſtament in verſe, was
the author and inventor of the Leonine verſes; but we
have reaſon to ſuppoſe that they were in vogue many
years before him.----See Diſſ. II. Hiſt. Engl. Poetry,
vol. 1.; and Du Cange's Gloſſary.

[g] In the caſe of moſt other conqueſts, the language of
a country has not been totally loſt, but mixed with that
of the conquerors; and out of that mixture a corrupt
language

the Latin language gave way to the foreign idioms of the Goths and Lombards, the pure and perfeſt ſtyle of the Roman tongue, corrupted and debaſed, loſt its original ſtrength and elegance. A mixed jargon of Latin, Celtic, and German, was all that remained ; which in the courſe of time, and by ſlow degrees, loſt its aſperity, and formed itſelf into the language of Italy : not ſoft and refined as at preſent (for that required long labour, and a milder diſpoſition), but rough and diſſonant. A long and dark night of ignorance ſucceeded. To books only could the learned refer, as the ſtores of Latin literature, to ſupport and propagate the

language produced. This was the caſe of the conqueſt of ſeveral provinces of the Roman empire by the northern nations. In Italy, for example, the language that took place after it was ſubdued by the Lombards, was a mixture of the Latin and the language of that people, which is the preſent Italian.

Origin and Progreſs of Language, vol. 1. p. 581.-

G   original

original language : but, alas! learned there were none who were capable of referring, and manuscripts very few which were known to have escaped the general wreck. In the year 501, Latin ceased totally to be spoken in Italy : the natives themselves, familiarized to foreign terms and expressions, no longer attempted to support their falling language. Ignorance and barbarity overshadowed alike the tongues and the hearts of man : nor was it till the introduction of established schools by Charlemagne that the clouds of darkness began to dispel; and a gleam, though faint, and scarce visible, shone on an unenlightened world. Churches and monasteries confined within their own walls the tender saplings of learning, which, for want of room to branch forth, soon withered and died. The pampered monks, " thriving on their fat pluralities," through indolence and ignorance, checked every communication

munication of liberal information; and, con-
tracted in their ideas of knowledge, chofe rather to indulge themfelves in the gloomy views
of fuperftition; than enjoy the profpect of revived literature, rifing as it were like the fun
from mift and clouds. Learning (to ufe the
words of an ingenious writer) was confidered
as dangerous to true piety; and darknefs was
neceffary to hide the ufurpations of the clergy,
who were then exalting themfelves on the ruins
of civil power. The ancient poets and orators
were reprefented as feducers to the paths of de-
ftruction; Virgil and Horace were the pimps
of Hell; Ovid a lecherous fiend; and Cicero
a vain declaimer, impioufly elated with the
talent of heathenifh reafoning. The circumfcribed notions of knowledge and literature
were entirely fwallowed up in logical treatifes
and uninterefting metaphyfics; the dry and ab-
ftrufe pages of Ariftotle were better fuited to

G 2   their

their dull and plodding difpofition: and, for near three centuries, thefe lazy and unedifying priefts were capable only of producing myfte-rious fyftems of theological fpeculation, or ufe-lefs difputations.——About the beginning of the feventh century, the gloom of fuperftitious ig-norance gave way to the light of rational in-ftruction.——The Arabs, who in the ravaging of the Afiatic provinces had refcued from deftruc-tion the works of fome of the moft eminent writers of Greece, by frequent incurfions into Europe, imported with them the principles of ufeful learning into a country totally dark and uninformed. In Spain and Africa univerfities were founded for the better propagation of ra-tional ftudies; and, by the liberal encourage-ment of Charlemagne, the weftern world be-came familiarized to the works of the Gre-cian and Roman writers.——In the beginning of the eleventh century, feveral profeffors from

the

the univerfities of Spain undertook the education of youth in Italy. Their method of inftruction comprehended the moſt numerous and uſeful ſciences; and was adapted to inſpire taſte and refinement, more than the perplexity of fcholaſtic diſputation. Before the year 1000, the monks of Mount Caſſino are ſaid to have diftinguiſhed themſelves not only for their knowledge of the ſciences, but their attention to polite literature, and an acquaintance with the claſſics. Tacitus Jornandes, Joſephus, Ovid's Faſti, Cicero, Seneca, Donatus the grammarian, Virgil, Theocritus, and Homer, had been collected by their learned abbot Deſiderius (or Didier [h]), who permitted the monks to

[h] He muſt not be confounded with Guillame de Saint Didier, a Provençal poet of the 12th century, who tranſlated the fables of Eſop into Provençal verſe. He wrote a treatiſe on fencing; and another on dreams, in which he laid down rules how they might be always true and

pleaſant.

to tranfcribe them.   Caffiodorus, who latterly belonged to this convent, had introduced among the monks the practice of copying manufcripts; and in the convent of St. Bennet a fixed portion of the day was fet apart, to be fpent entirely in this very laudable exercife. But indolence had fo infenfibly crept upon them, that in the ninth and tenth centuries this occupation was neglected, for the fole purpofe of compofing pious legends, unedifying homilies, and the lives of faints and martyrs.   To Defiderius it was left to procure new copies, and revife the old.   This illuftrious man (afterwards Pope, under the name of Victor III.) was elect-

pleafant.   The fecret confifted in not loading the ftomach, left the grofs fumes rifing up to the head, fhould caufe melancholy ideas.   The works of the abbot Didier are, Dialogorum Libri Quatuor de Miraculis S. Benedicti, aliorumque Monachorum in Monafterio Caffinenfi---Cantus quidam de S. Mauro, abbate Caffinenfi---Epiftolæ ad Diverfos.---See Poffevinus, vol. i. p. 458.

ed

ed Abbot in 1058. His zeal for the caufe of religion and literature, his refined tafte for the polite arts, and his munificence in fupporting them, will ever reflect the higheft honor both on his head and heart. So liberal was he to his fociety, that he not only procured for them books in every fcience and every language, but rebuilt both the church and monaftery, in a ftyle truly magnificent. From all parts of Italy he collected architects, fculptors, painters; and artifts fkilled in mofaic work, in marble; gold, filver, and ivory; and from Greece the inlayers of marble for the pavements; and he alfo had the art taught to his monks.—Jerome, abbot of Pompofa, towards the end of the eleventh century, followed the example of Defiderius, in amaffing books. An account of his labours in the caufe of literature was pub-lifhed by P. Montfaucon.—In 1053, an Italian, named Papias, publifhed a Latin dictionary,

which,

which, although defective in many parts, con‐
tains some curious information [i]. — The monks
of Caffino, far from devoting all their time to
tranfcribing, began to circulate among them‐
felves little pieces of poetry, and by degrees to
compofe larger works. — William of Pouillé
wrote a poem in five books, as a hiftory of the
Normans, from their arrival in Italy to the death
of the celebrated Robert Guifchard. — Alfanus,
archbifhop of Salerna, is the only one whofe
works we are acquainted with. — Another poe‐
tical hiftorian was Donizon, a prieft and monk
of Canoffa, who wrote in verfe the Life of the
Countefs Matilda, from her birth. — The num‐
ber of thofe who, about the year 1183, ap‐
plied themfelves to the ftudy of Latin poetry

---

[i] Benedictus, monachus Caffinenfis clarus, circa A. 1060,.
fcripfit Hiftoriam S. Secundini, Epifcopi Trojani, in Apu‐
liâ; quæ, cum Hymnis in eundem Secundinum, exftat apud:
Ughellum.—Fabricii Bibl. Med. Æt. iv. p. 555.

in

in Italy, is extremely limited; but thofe who
wrote verfes merely for chants, fervices, and other
pious offices, are too numerous to be comprehended in this short view.—In the 13th century, whilft the fpirit of claffical Latin poetry
was univerfally prevailing, our countryman
(fays Mr. Warton) Geoffrey de Vinefauf, an
accomplifhed fcholar, and educated not only
in the priory of St. Fridefwide in Oxford, but
in the univerfities of France and Italy (he was
a profeffor at Bologna), publifhed, while at
Rome, a critical didactic poem, intitled, " De
Novâ Poeticâ. This book is dedicated to Pope
Innocent III. and its intention was to recom-
mend and illuftrate the new and legitimate
mode of verfification which had lately begun to
flourifh in Europe, in oppofition to the Leonine or barbarous fpecies."—Stefanardo de
Vimercate, a prieft diftinguifhed for his learning (the firft who was elected Profeffor of Theology

ology in the cathedral of Milan), wrote the history of Archbifhop Otto Vifconti, in Latin verfe; which, confidering the age, was pure and elegant. Richard, judge of Venoza, wrote an elegiac poem, De Nuptiis; and James de Benevento was the author of fome Carmina Moralia, preferved in MS. in the library of the Marquis Ricardi at Florence.— After thefe an unknown author wrote fome epigrams, De Balneis Pozzalanicis.—At this period the foreign languages were taught in Italy; and the Greek and Arabic, whence they tranflated the works of Ariftotle and other philofophers, became a neceffary ftudy. Hebrew alfo was among their literary accomplifhments.—John of Capua, about the year 1262, tranflated from the Hebrew his Directorium Vitæ Humanæ, which he fays was tranflated from the Indian language into the Perfian, thence into Arabic, and from the

Arabic

Arabic into the Hebrew. This Directorium contains the well-known Culila & Dimna, five Στεφανιτην και Ιχνηλατην, a collection of fayings, part true, and part fabulous, on moral and civil fubjects, and contains inftruction for courtiers.

. It cannot be fuppofed that, in this fhort fketch, I can mention every one who wrote either in Latin verfe or profe, before Petrarch; fuffice it therefore to name one, whofe exertions in the caufe of literature have been but little known, and lefs praifed. The moft illuftrious therefore of all thofe who wrote their hiftories in Latin, was Albertino Muffato [k], the

[k] The name and writings of Muffato were hardly known till they were brought forward to the public . notice in the Effay on Pope, which I fhall not be accufed of partiality (as I only join the voice of the world) in calling the moft agreeable and judicious piece of criticifm produced by the prefent age.

Hift. of Eng. Poetry, vol. ii. p. 400.

hiftorian

historian of Padua, eminently skilled in history, poetry, and eloquence : he was born in the year 1261. The loss of his father when he was young, the charge of a numerous family, and the poverty which seemed to threaten him, were the source of innumerable difficulties. In this situation he gained a scanty income by copying manuscripts for the scholars of the university; and, having considerable practice, he naturally imbibed a taste for literature. His acute genius beginning to expand and display its powers, gained him great patronage; and his deep knowledge of law procured him reputation and riches. In the year 1325, after having borne many considerable offices, and served in defence of his country, he was banished to Chiozza, where he died, very old, in 1329. In his exile he amused himself with revising and finishing his historical works. The first he calls Historia Augusta; containing, in sixteen books,

books, the life and actions of the emperor Henry the Seventh, to whom he was fent as ambaſſador by the Paduans fix different times: in his hiſtory he has inſerted all his ſpeeches before this prince, and in the ſenate at Padua. His ſecond was a kind of record of the events in Italy, but particularly in Padua, under the Great Can della Scala, and the conſequences of his expedition. The third contained a relation of the methods uſed by the Great Can to gain the government of Padua.—When he had finiſhed theſe works, he ſketched out a Life of Louis de Bavaria, but death ſtopped his progreſs.—All theſe hiſtories were written with truth and eloquence: and, as the critics obſerve, if in his ſtyle he had added purity and elegance, Padua would have boaſted of a ſecond Livy.

Muſſato was ſo highly honored for his abilities, that the biſhop of Padua crowned him publicly

licly with laurel; and iffued an edict, that on
every Chriftmas day the doctors, regents, and
profeffors of the two colleges in that city, fhould
go to his houfe in folemn proceffion, with wax
tapers in their hands, and offer him a triple
crown [1].—As I have fpoken of him only as an
hiftorian, it is but proper to mention him as the
chief reftorer of Latin poetry. His three books
of the Siege of Padua — his Eclogues, Elegies,
Epitaphs, Hymns—and his two tragedies, Ecer-
rinis and Achilleis, the firft of which is the fate
of Ecerinus, tyrant of Padua—are evident
marks of poetical talents. To fuppofe that
thefe tragedies are conducted with the proper
rules of unity and time, although on the plan of
the Greek drama, would be abfurd; fince they
are but bad copies of their bad original, Seneca.
To fpeak the truth then, however they have

[1] By another decree, public lectures were inftituted on
his hiftorical and poetical works.

been

been faid to be the firft regular tragedies fince the barbarous ages, they are, uninterefting, poor, and inconfiderable.—But to Muffato the greateft praife is due for attempting to revive and reanimate the flumbering fpirit of tragedy, buried under the gloom of ignorance for fo many ages. To a man therefore whofe merits are fo little acknowledged, I feel a pleafure in communicating my tribute of praife, trifling as it is, and in mentioning a name fo confpicu- ous in the annals of modern learning. The ftudy of the Italian language in the univerfities proceeded from difpofition and tafte; that of the Latin, from a fenfe of its fuperiority, and a defire of reputation. It was not his Sonnets that procured Petrarch the diftinguifhed honour of being crowned in the Capitol—it was to his Latin poem " Africa," his Eclogues, and Epiftles, that he owed all his glory.—From the reftorers of the Latin tongue. Petrarch is

fuppofed

suppofed to have received all his knowledge in that language : but to his capacious mind, which could not be bounded by the narrow view of modern Latinity, the images of the Roman writers ever appeared.   Animated with the flight acquaintance with their works, and difappointed at the ufelefs labours of bad copy-ifts, he determined to collect from foreign countries the beft copies that remained of the writers of the Auguftan age.   In the 11th cen-tury, although public feminaries and univerfi-ties were founded, books were fo extremely dear and fcarce, that it was in the power of but few men to fupport the expence of maintaining and paying copyifts.   The pay of thefe copy-ifts was fo expenfive, that the fortunes of pri-vate perfons could not afford them an oppor-tunity of multiplying books.   It was the tafte of the times to ornament with gold the capital letters of every word, and to illumi-

nate

nate the margins with the richeſt and moſt profuſe colouring ᵐ.. Miſſals and breviaries were the only books on which they exerciſed their talent. In that age the word *library* was often given to a ſmall collection of duplicate Bibles. To give an idea of a library in thoſe days, I will add a catalogue of the books of Cardinal Guala, left by will to the monaſtery of St. Andrew, founded by him at Vercelli : A large Bible written in French, bound in purple, ornamented with flowers of gold, and capital letters richly gilt; another Bible bound in blue

---

ᵐ Hodie ſcriptores non ſunt ſcriptores, ſed pictores, ſays Sarti, in his Hiſtory of the Univerſity of Bologna; ſince the luxury of literature confiſted in ſplendid embelliſhments, not in the intrinſic value of the books. At Milan there were fifty copyiſts; and at Bologna a great number, who in writing and painting had great merit; but, as they regarded beauty more than correctneſs, we may imagine that errors unavoidably crept into the text.

H   leather;

leather; another in red; a fourth in Englifh;
a fifth very fmall, but valuable, in French
characters of gold, and ornamented with purple; the books of Exodus and Leviticus in
old characters; the twelve prophets in one volume, in Lombard letters; St. Gregory's books
of morality, in very legible old letters of Arezzo.
—This was a library which, for fcarcity and
value, was confidered as an ineftimable trea-
fure.—The collection of Cervotto Accurfo was
in great reputation at Bologna, although it confifted only of twenty volumes of Law.

At the time of Petrarch, near two centuries after, the fame complaint was made
of the fcarcenefs of books, and the incorrect-
nefs of tranfcribers. How, fays he, in one
of his Dialogues[n], can we remedy the faults of
thefe copyifts, who by ignorance and indolence hurt the caufe of literature? Whoever

---

[n] De rem. utriufque fort. lib. i. dial. 43.

.can

can paint on parchment, and hold a pen,
passes among us for an eminent tranfcriber,
though perhaps he has neither fenfe nor talents. If Livy, Cicero, or Pliny particularly,
could rife from their graves, and perufe their
mutilated works, would they not affirm that
what they read was not their own, but that of
fome barbarian? And, in a letter to Boccacio,
he complains that he could find no one who
could faithfully tranfcribe his treatife De
Vitâ Solitariâ; and adds, that it is aftonifhing that a book, which was written in a few
months, fhould fcarcely be copied in as many
years. The only fource which was left, was
to collate and correct thofe manufcripts which
were generally known, and to fearch for
others yet undifcovered. Petrarch, Boccacio, and Collucio, diftinguifhed themfelves
in this kind of literary labour. To correct
dates, and determine upon the exact time in

which each author lived, was a work as neceſ-
ſary as it was difficult; ſince, in a letter to a
learned man of Meſſina, Petrarch diſcovers his
ignorance in ſuppoſing that Cicero and Plato
were poets, that Ennius and Statius were con-
temporaries; and in not knowing that Nevius
and Plautus ever exiſted. To ſeparate truth
from fable, to prune and lop off the interpola-
tions of commentators, and to purge from
barbariſms and faults the original text, demand-
ed the utmoſt attention; and laſtly, to diſcover
the traces of any remains of antiquity, required
labour and money.—In all theſe ſeveral particulars, literature found a firm and perſevering
friend in Petrarch. The numerous acquaintance which he had in France, Italy, Spain,
Germany, Greece, England, and Scotland,
offered their aſſiſtance. But, to ſhew more no-
bly his unremitting zeal in the cauſe of ſcience,
he travelled into foreign countries, and never

mitted

omitted to fearch the libraries of ancient monafteries for unknown manufcripts. By thefe
means he difcovered copies of books which he
had never feen ; and, by the help of others, he
corrected thofe which he was in poffeffion of.
In all thefe refearches Petrarch found only the
Orations and Familiar Letters of Cicero, and
a bad copy of Quintilian : the honour of difco-
vering a perfect copy of this writer, fo little
known, was referved for Poggius; who acquaints us, in one of his letters written from
Conftance in 1417, that, in the bottom of a
tower of the monaftery of St. Gall °, he met
with

* Quintilian fut racheté a Bafle des mains d'un Char-
cutier, pendant le concile qui s'y tenoit; et le feul exemplaire original qu'on en ait jamais vu. Agobard
(archbifhop of Lyons in the ninth century) fut trouvé
a Lyon chez un relieur par Papire le Maffon.—Maf-
fo publifhed this manufcript at Paris, in 1603, in 8vo;
and the original was, after his death, depofited by his

H 3   brother

with this invaluable author, together with the
three first books of Valerius Flaccus's Argo-
                                        nautica,

brother in the king of France's library.   An improved
edition was publifhed at Paris, in two vols. 8vo, in 1666,
by Mr. Baluze.—I cannot forbear adding the following
anecdote from the fame author. Le Gòverneur de feu
M. de Marquis de Rouville jouant a là longue paume
dans une terre pres de Saumur, lut par hazard ce qui
etoit ecrit fur le parchemin dè fon batoir, & reconnut
que c'etoit une feuille dè fa feconde decade de Tite
Live.   Il courut en meme tems chez le faifeur de batoirs,
qui lui dit qu'il n'y avoit pas longtems qu'il avoit em-
ploié la derniere feuille.—Menagiana, tom. iii. p. 167.—
Le Pogge avoit en effet trouvé chez un vendeur des falines,
le real exemplaire, qui etoit refte des ouvrages de ce fameux auteur (fpeaking of Quintilian), & il avant rendu public—fays the ingenious author of the Characters of Ancient and Modern Writers; but on what authority I know
not. The very copy of Quintilian, which Poggius found,
belonged to Lord Sunderland, whofe valuable library is
now at Blenheim.   Of Tacitus the fame author fays,
Les cinq premiers livres des Annales de Tacite avoient ete
recouvrez dans la monaftere de Corbie, fur la Vezer en
                                        Allemagne;

nautica, and Asconius Pedianus's Comments on eight Orations of Tully[p]. The Familiar Epiftles of Cicero, which Petrarch found, were the fource of the greateft pleafure that he ever received. That he fpared no expence in this fearch, is very evident from many parts of his letters, and particularly from 'this—Quoties pecuniam mifi, non per Italiam modò ubi eram notior, fed per Gallias atque Germaniam, et ufque ad Hifpanias atque Britanniam : dicam quod mireris, et in Græciam mifi ; et unde Ciceronem expectabam, habui Homerum.

Allemagne ; que Leon X. n'avoit jamais recu un prefent plus agreable puifque celui qui le lui fit, eut cinq cens ecus d'or pour recompenfe ; et que Come de Medicis, un des plus fages princes de fon temps, s'etoit formé fur les maximes de cet incomparable politique.

[p] This very ancient manufcript, with a copy written by Petrarch himfelf, together with the Epiftles to Atticus, and works of Virgil, is preferved in the Laurentine library at Florence.

Concerning

Concerning the firft introduction of Homer
into Italy, Boccacio⁹, I believe, is fuppofed to
have

⁹ This great man vifited Petrarch at Venice, in 1363;
and carried with him Leontius Pilatus of Theffalonica,
a man of genius, but of haughty temper, whom Petrarch ftyles Magna Bellua. From this fingular man,
who perifhed in a voyage from Conftantinople to Venice (he was ftruck with lightning while clinging to
the maft), Petrarch received a Latin tranflation of the
Iliad and Odyffey. To thefe words of a learned critic let us add, that, from the account which the Abbé
de Sade gives of thefe tranflations, we are led to fuppofe that Leontius Pilatus never finifhed the Odyffey;
whereas a perfect copy of thefe tranflations is preferved
in the library of the Benedictines at Florence, as writ-
tᶜn by Pilatus, and copied afterwards by Nicolas Ni-
li. The miftake therefore is this: Petrarch did not
receive it from Pilatus himfelf, but from Boccacio; whom
Petrarch befeeches, in the following words, to fend him
as quick as poffible the remainder of the Odyffey—
Poftremo autem, ne amici volatilis (fpeaking of Pilatus
who had left him) tam verbofa mentio fruftra fit, redit
hic in animum, te precari, ut Homericæ partem illam
Odyffeæ

have the reputation of firſt circulating copies of the divine bard. ˝Notwithſtanding his po-

Odyſſeæ qua Ulyſſes it ad inferos, et locos qui in veſ-tibulo Erebi ſunt deſcriptionem ab Homero factam----ab hoc autem, de quo agimus---tuo hortatu in Lati-num verſam, mihi quam primum potes, admodum egenti, utcunque tuis digitis enarratam mittas. Hoc in preſens: in futurum autem, ſi me amas, vide, obſecro, an tuo ſtudio, meâ impenſâ, fieri pöſſit, ut Homerus integer bibliothecæ huic, ubi pridem Græcus habitat, tandem Latinus accedat.---Epiſt. V. Rer. Sen. lib. iii.---From Boc-cacio, much about the time of this viſit, Petrarch re-ceived a copy of St. Auguſtin's Expoſitio in Pſalmos, preſerved in the king of France's library, in which is this memorandum in

Petrarch's Hand Writing:

De Re Diplomatica.

verty,

verty, and gay difpofition, it is aftonifhing
that he had either leifure or inclination to
tranfcribe himfelf fo many copies of the Greek
and Roman writers, which, by paffing through
his hands, were purged from blunders and in-
accuracies, and gained confiderable refinement
and purity.

While thefe learned men were exert-
ing themfelves in procuring manufcripts, and
were rendering themfelves immortal by their
own productions, many bars were yet in the
way of literature. One obftruction, which I
confider to be the greateft, was the exceffive
dearnefs of parchment; and, as a proof, take
the following anecdote : Petrarque habille d'une
fimple vefte de cuir paffe, ecrivoit fur elle les
penfes qu'il craignoit de perdre, a proportion
qu' elles fe prefentoient a fon efprit. Cette vefte
pleine d'ecriture, & couverte de ratures, etoit
encore en 1527 confervée, & refpecta comme
un

en monument precieux de litterature par Jacque
Sadolet, Jean Cafa, & Louis Bucatello, noms
fameux dans la republique des lettres : la veneration qu'on avoit pour les livres de St.
Athanafe faifoit dire à un Abbé qu'au defaut
de papier, il faloit les ecrire fur fes habits ʳ.
Through the want of materials to write on,
many manufcripts of the eighth, ninth, and following centuries, are ftill extant, wrote on
parchment from which fome former writing had
been erafed, in order to fubftitute a new compofition in its place.   And in this manner (fays
an intelligent hiftorian) it is probable that
feveral works of the ancients perifhed : a book
of Livy, or of Tacitus, might be erafed to
make room for the legendary tale of a faint,
or the fuperftitious prayers of a miffal.   This
very eafily accounts for the fmall number of
manufcripts of the Grecian or Roman authors

ʳ This reminds us of Hogarth, who would frequently fketch faces on his nails.

during

during thofe and fucceeding ages.—The fcarcity of books has been proved by many cir-
cumftances, fince private perfons feldom pof-
feffed any, 'and even monafteries of confiderable note had only one miffal°. To remedy

° The countefs of Anjou purchafed a copy of the Homilies of Haimon bifhop of Halberftadt, by paying two
hundred fheep, five quarters of millet, five of rye, and
five of wheat.—Hiftoire Literaire de France, tom. vii. p. 3.

In the library which Charles the Fifth founded in
France, about the year 1376, among many books of
devotion, aftrology, chemiftry, and romance, there was
not one copy of Tully to be found, and no Latin poet
but Ovid, Lucan, and Boethius; fome French tranflations
of Livy, Valerius Maximus, and St. Auftin's City of
God.—Effay on Pope, vol. ii. p. 11.

. Le Prince Jean, duc de Berri, avoit herité de fon
frere Charles V. un grand goût pour les livres. Il fe
forma une bibliotheque dont le catalogue contient environ cent volumes. Ce font des Bibles, des Pfeautiers,
des Heures, des traduétions de quelques traités parti-
culiers des faints Peres, des Hiftoires anciennes, mo-
dernes, romanefques, &c. Il falloit des trefors pour
faire

medy this misfortune, Petrarch, Boccacio, and Salutato earneſtly ſolicited their friends to procure them copies whole or mutilated. Petrarch ſpeaks of his library with raptures, calling it his treaſure, his joy, and conſolation. He had in his old age offered it to the ſtate of Venice, where a building was prepared for it; but, being fickle and inconſtant, he altered his mind, and gave part of it to Donato de Carantino, but in the greateſt perfection, as ſome of his books were ſcattered abroad, and fell in-

faire une ſemblable collection. Le prix en eſt marqué dans ce catalogue; et on y trouve " des Bibles qui ont coûté, trois cent livres; un traité de la Cite de Dieu, deux cens livres; un Tite Live, cent trente-cinq livres:" et ainſi des autres. Les copiſtes avoient trouvé l'art d'embellir les livres de mille ornemens riches, et d'un travail fort recherché; ce qui les rendoit beaucoup plus chers & plus rares, parce que le tems qu'ils qu'ils mettoient a embellir leur ecriture, n'etoit pas employé à copier.—Anecdotes Françoiſes, p. 299.

to

to other hands. —The library of Boccacio was more fortunate in its possessors; since he left it by will to the Augustine Convent at Florence, where it has been carefully preserved. That of Salutato, which consisted of six hundred volumes, a prodigious collection for those times, was, at his death, sold in small lots by his children.—The palaces of princes, and religious houses, following the example of these learned men, were shortly after furnished with manuscripts. Robert, king of Naples, was the first who collected the works of the Greek and Roman writers; and the convents of the Cordeliers, Dominicans, and Augustines at Florence, were highly proud of their valuable literary acquisitions. The monks of Mount Cassino, so celebrated for their manuscripts in the 11th century, had, on the contrary, lost their taste for polite studies. Boccacio, who went to visit that library, with the hopes no doubt of discovering

covering something valuable, says that he was astonished to find the books torn, mouldy, trampled on the ground, and covered with filth; and that a monk told him it was owing to the ignorance and avarice of his brethren. However difficult the access to Greek and Roman writers was in the time of Petrarch, yet by the assistance of Quintilian, imperfect as it was—of Virgil—and more particularly of Cicero, whom he mentions frequently as the source of all his information, Petrarch cultivated successfully a talent for Latin composition. His style cannot be supposed to be that of Tully or Livy; as it is often unnecessarily diffuse, sometimes cramp, and frequently confused by circumlocution, and bewildered by digression : yet there is a certain smoothness and polished volubility, which we look for in vain in works prior to his (excepting those of Muffato), and which seems to have thrown off the oppressive shackles

of

of scholaftic barbarifm.   His Africa, his
Eclogues, and Epiftles, inferior certainly to
Virgil in beauty of expreffion and harmony of
verfe, are infinitely fuperior to all writers after the fifth century.—It would be a work of
much labour, to compare with the writings
of Petrarch the Latin authors of his age, and
to point out every paffage of his poems in
which the ftyle and expreffions of Virgil have
been judicioufly or injudicioufly copied ; fince
it will be fufficient to fay that, by his attentive
reading of the pureft Latin authors, and by his
quick and vigorous imagination, he acquired
a flow of words, and a method of arrangement,
which gave him this evident fuperiority.   It
was, as before obferved, entirely owing to this
talent that he was prefented in fo confpicuous a
manner with the laureate's crown ; and fo valuable did the ftudy of the Latin language appear
to the more enlightened part of mankind, that
                                    the

the very corpfe of Colucio Salutato was publick-
ly crowned by the Florentines.   The abilities
of Convenevole del Prato[t], who was Petrarch's
mafter at Avignon, of Muffato, of Bonato, of
Zanobi del Strada[w], Lovato del Padua[x], and

[t] He was a native of Prato in Tufcany.   At Avignon
he was Profeffor of Grammar for fixty years, but on his
return to Prato was prefented with the crown.

[w] This Florentine poet was an intimate friend of Petrarch, who procured for him the place of Chief Juf-
tice of Naples.   In the year 1355, the emperor Charles
the Fourth, in a folemn affembly, crowned him with his
own hands, and afterwards conducted him through
every ftreet of Pifa, with the laurel wreath on his head.
Zanobi is faid to have had the complexion and deli-
cacy of a woman, joined to an extreme referve and
modefty.   His converfation was agreeable, and his
countenance always ferene and fmiling.   His works are
loft.   He died of the plague in 1361.

[x] He had written the laws of the twelve tables in
verfe, and feveral pieces, but his works are perifhed.
He is by miftake called Donato by Petrarch and Fabricius.

I   Cardinal

Cardinal Stefanefchi ᵞ gained them the fame honor; but unfortunately we cannot judge of their merits, as moſt of their poems are either loſt, or preſerved only in manuſcript, in the cabinets of the curious. Their names, and the accounts we have of them, are ſufficient proofs that the ſtudy of Latin literature was firmly eſtabliſhed in Italy during the time of Petrarch, who is univerſally allowed to have exerted himſelf moſt powerfully in the for- faken caufe of literature.

ᵞ He was created cardinal by Boniface the Eight. He wrote three ſhort Latin poems on the abdication of Celeſtin V. and the creation of Boniface. He died at Avignon, 1343.

F I N I S.

Governor

Governor Phillip's Voyage to Botany Bay.

This Day is published, Price 1*l.* 11*s* 6*d.* in Boards,

Or with the Natural Hiſtory coloured, 2*l.* 12s. 6*d.*

In One large Volume, Quarto, printed on fine Paper, and embelliſhed with upwards of FIFTY COPPER PLATES,

The Maps and Charts taken from actual Surveys, and the Plans and Views drawn on the Spot, by Capt. HUNTER, Lieut. SHORTLAND, Lieut. WATTS, Lieut. DAWES, Lieut. BRADLEY, Capt. MARSHALL, &c.

And Engraved by

MEDLAND, SHERWIN, MAZELL, HARRISON, &c.

THE VOYAGE OF GOVERNOR PHILLIP TO BOTANY BAY; with an Account of the ESTABLISHMENT of the COLONIES at PORT JACKSON and NORFOLK ISLAND; compiled from Authentic Papers, which have been received from the ſeveral Departments.

To which are added,

The JOURNALS of Lieut. SHORTLAND of the *Alexander*: Lieut. WATTS of the *Penrhyn*; Lieut. BALL of the *Supply*; and Capt. MARSHALL of the *Scarborough*; with an Account of their New Diſcoveries.

LONDON : Printed for JOHN STOCKDALE, Piccadilly.

The following is a Liſt of ſome of the Engravings which are in this Work:

1 Head of Governor Phillip, from a Painting in the Poſſeſſion of Mr. Nepean, by F. Wheatley ; engraved by Sherwin

2 Head of Lieut. Shortland, engraved by Sherwin, from a Painting of Shelley's

3 Head

Books published for John Stockdale.

3 Head of Lieut. King, from a Painting by Wright
4 View of Botany Bay, with the Supply and Sirius at Anchor, and the Transports coming in
5 A large Chart of Port Jackson
6 A View in Port Jackson, with the Natives in their Canoes trouling
7 View of the Natives in Botany Bay.
8 Map of Lord Howe Island.
9 View of ditto
10 View of Natives and a Hut in New South Wales
11 View of New South Wales
12 A large Plan of the Establishment at Sydney Cove, Port Jackson
13 A large Chart of Norfolk Island
14 View of Ball's Pyramid
15 Chart of Lieut. Shortland's new Discoveries
16 Track of the Alexander from Port Jackson to Batavia.
17 Chart of Capt. Marshall's new Discoveries
18 View of the Natives in their sailing Canoe at Mulgrave's Islands
19 View of Curtis's Island
20 View of Macauley's Island
21 Caspian Tern
22 The Kangaroo
23 The Spotted Opossum
24 Vulpine Opossum
25 Norfolk Island Flying Squirrel
26 Blue Bellied Parrot
27 Tabuan Parrot
28 Pennanthian Parrot
29 Pacific Parrot
30 Sacred King's Fisher
31 Superb Warbler, male
32 Superb Warbler, female
33 Norfolk Island Petrel
34 Bronze-winged Pigeon
35 White-fronted Hern
36 Wattled Bea-eater

37 Pttsitaceous

37 Psittaceous Hornbill
38 Martin Cat
39 Kanguroo Rat
40 A Dog of New South Wales
41 The Black Cockatoo
42 Red-shouldered Parrakeet
43 Watt's Shark
44 The Laced Lizard
45 New Holland Goat Sucker
46 White Gallinule
47 New Holland Cassowary
48 Port Jackson Shark

N. B. Gentlemen desirous of having fine Impressions are requested to send as early as possible to the Publisher, or to their respective Booksellers.

Most of the Non-descript Quadrupeds, Reptiles, Birds Fish, &c. from which the Drawings are taken, may be seen at the Publisher's.

Also published this Day,

A VOYAGE ROUND THE WORLD, but more paricularly to the NORTH-WEST COAST OF AMERICA; performed in 1785, 1786, 1787, and 1788, in the KING GEORGE ;

(Dedicated, by Permission, to HIS MAJESTY)

By CAPTAIN NATHANIEL PORTLOCK.

Neatly printed in One large Volume, Royal Quarto, and embellished with Twenty elegant Copper Plates. Printed on fine Paper, hot-pressed, and Plates coloured, Price only 1l. 11s. 6d. in Boards, or ou common Paper, 1l. 5s. in Boards.

N. B. Gentlemen desirous of having fine Impressions are requested to send as early as possible to the Publisher, or to their respective Booksellers.

SHAKSPEARE,

SHAKSPEARE, with a complete INDEX.

***

In the Prefs, and fpeedily will be publifhed,

In One large Volume Octavo, containing near 1500 Pages, printed upon. a fine Royal Paper, and embcllifhed with a Head of the Author,

S H A K S P E A R E,

Including, in One Volume, the WHOLE of his DRAMATIC WORKS; with EXPLANATORY NOTES, compiled from various Commentators.

To which will be firft added

A copious INDEX to all the remarkable PASSAGES and WORDS, calculated to point out the different Meanings in which the Words are made ufe of by Shakfpeare:

By the Rev. SAMUEL AYSCOUGH, F. A. S.

And Affiftant Librarian of the Britifh Mufeum.

*** The want of an Index to all the beautiful and remarkable Paffages in Shakfpeare has long been regretted, but the difficulty of the undertaking has hitherto prevented every attempt. Mr. Stockdale has already experienced a liberal encouragement from the Public for his Edition of Shakfpeare, in one Volume 8vo. and to whom he begs leave to return his grateful acknowlcdgments. As the prefent edition will coft him near 2000l. he humbly folicits the affiftance of the Admirers of Shakfpeare, by favouring him with their names as Subfcribers.

A Lift of the Encouragers of a Work which is intended to make this favourite Author ftill more ufeful and agreeable, will be prefixed.

The price to Subfcribers 1l. 5s. to Non-Subfcribers 1l. 10s.

www.ingramcontent.com/pod-product-compliance
Lightning Source LLC
Chambersburg PA
CBHW032016010726
47493CB00007B/2423